BACK END
OF THE
BELL CURVE

TALES OF THE
UNCOMMONLY UNLUCKY

BACK END
OF THE
BELL CURVE

TALES OF THE
UNCOMMONLY UNLUCKY

PHILL BRADLEY

Dark Matter Publishing LLC

ISBN: 979-8-9916964-0-1 (eBook)
ISBN: 979-8-9916964-1-8 (Paperback)

Library of Congress Control Number: 2024921403

These stories are works of fiction. Any references to historical events, real people, or real places are used fictitiously. Names, characters, and places are products of the author's imagination, and any resemblance to actual events or persons or places, living or dead, is entirely coincidental.

Editing: David Yurkovich
Cover design: Farah @fagraphy

First printing edition 2024.

Dark Matter Publishing LLC
1804 Ballinger Dr.
Spicewood, TX 78669
www.phillbradley.com

for Shellie, Bix, and Brooke

Special Thanks

Angela Yuriko Smith for mentoring

David Yurkovich for editing

Content/Trigger Warnings

The works in this collection contain elements of horror, violence, or death. And while many readers prefer to be surprised, some readers may have an adverse reaction to specific types of content.

For all stories, please expect adult violence and death on par with a rated R movie or MA television show.

I have included keys to special types of content in the annotated table of contents so the reader may easily avoid certain types of stories.

Genre

While most of the works in this collection contain elements of horror, some may disagree that many of these stories are really horror genre writing.

I have included a key in the annotated table of contents to allude to the following subgenres: BOD (Body horror), THR (Thriller), PSY (Psychological horror), SPEC (Speculative fiction), SCI (Science fiction), HIS (Historical fiction), and COM (Comedy).

Consider the genre of speculative fiction as things that could be. Not the hard science of sci-fi, but more like supernatural occurrences, non-human monsters, and life after death. Maybe these things do exist; they're here for me to present and for you to decide.

Contents

Genres

BOD - Body horror
COM - Comedy
HIS - Historical fiction
PSY - Psychological horror
SCI - Science fiction
SPEC - Speculative fiction
THR – Thriller

Warnings

AC – Animal cruelty, may be implied
CHI – Children are involved
FIR – Fire
GOR – Gore, blood, guts
GRS – Gross-out
GUN – Guns, used violently
MEN – Mental health, esp. degenerative
RAC – Racism
RAP – Rape
REL – Religion
SUI – Suicide
SUB – Substance abuse

PREFACE

Ever since I was a young child, I've had very vivid dreams and daydreams with clear dialog and settings and smells and colors. And it's not uncommon for anything at all to trigger a fantasy: a phrase, a mishap, a wish. It's similar to Thurber's "The Secret Life of Walter Mitty," but usually it's other people in the fantasies, and that's who I write about.

Over the years I've gotten better at recording my thoughts: I text myself ideas to remember, I collate dozens of categorized lists in Excel, and I write. Writing is a way for me to take an idea and make something meaningful out of it: maybe an invention I will never patent or manufacture, or maybe a funny thought that could brighten someone's day, or even my own day, down the road. And it's a sense of closure that I haven't squandered that idea which may never come again.

For me, part of the fun of writing for a living is to keep learning. Some of this manifests itself in science fiction, but also in historical fiction, and details from world-wide locations, customs, and peoples. I relish doing the research so the tales feel authentic. I'm sure you picked up this book to be entertained, but you also might learn something about scuba diving, or Paraguay, or skinny-ass horses.

I wasn't always a writer – as a kid, and younger adult, I leaned on math and science, seeking the "right answers." But through my non-writing career I found out you need a little bit of persuasion to go along with facts and figures and a good story is sometimes as important as the right answer. Conversely, I've found the more I write, that there is a science to it – ways to say things that are effective and provide the reader with a wonderful experience.

I still love science and technology, but I don't think they hold all the answers we seek. Sometimes we have to fill in the gaps with hope and faith. That's where speculative fiction comes in. Sometimes you just have to make up the answers. And the questions.

I've often seen the advice, "Write what you know." Well, I think what I know is that we know nothing. Crazy, inexplicable stuff happens all the time.

When I start writing a story, I usually have some nugget of warped inspiration, but no details. I rarely have a beginning, middle, or end in mind. The stories just flow out, and I have to make decisions about what's going to happen. I like being surprised and I hope you do too.

For me the short story format is my bread and butter. I love the sense of accomplishment and get the same high finishing a 500-word short story as an 80,000-word novel. So why not? I also love the technicality of getting everything into the story efficiently – getting the reader to love the characters in a very short timeframe, setting up the plot and having a satisfying ending, with a little bit of foreshadowing and flashbacks for good measure.

Not everyone dies in my stories, but I've chosen this group of stories for my introductory collection because the characters all face challenges that change or end their lives. Some of them make bad decisions, with brutal consequences. Some of them are just dealt a poor hand of fate.

And is it horror, or thriller, or speculative, or sci-fi, or something else? I don't know. All I want to do is write entertaining stories. I hope you like these and are entertained.

HENRY THE HORSE

Henry the Horse was constantly being bullied by the mustangs and other stallions at the horse farm. When they were in the stable, the neighboring horses would pee on his hay, and when they were in the corral, they would kick dirt in his face and make fun of his skinny physique and thin mane.

One day Henry decided to run away. He made a break for it when the corral gate was closing, headed across the meadow, and barely cleared the three-foot fence at the edge of the property.

It started to rain, but just when he was almost out of energy, he saw a gray metal building. *Shelter*. He made it to the building and slept just under the eave. In the morning, some humans found Henry, and he heard them say, "He seems to be a stray; we better take care of him," which really lifted his spirits until everything went black and he was made into ground meat for $1.99 a pound. Other horses got $2.99 a pound, but not Henry.

THE FALL

Garrett called out from the back room, "Guys, put it on channel 10. They're showing that gymnast dude who died at the WAAC."

Eddie and I changed the channel: supposedly some guy fell over 200 stories during the World Aerial Athletics Championships. This event was pretty popular due to the danger element: guys and gals doing parkour on cranes and giant robots, called grobots, used to build massive skyscrapers in places like Doha and Hyderabad. To date, no one had died. Even though there were several falls, the sport employed a technology where most of the participants wore suits fitted with magnetics. Safety drones with large electromagnets had caught a dozen or more unlucky athletes, usually within the first few meters of the fall. However, in this case, one of the top competitors, a skilled Latvian named Ralfs Ozols, wore his own trademark all-white, non-magnetic form-fitting suit, which had started a fashion craze all around the world. Ralfs cited the rigidity, the weight, and the slight pull on metal apparatus as reasons for not wanting to wear the safety suit.

Ozols was a well-proportioned man, with high cheekbones and spiky blonde hair; his look, a marketing dream, though he preferred to lead a private life, shunning the media and keeping to himself. His interviews were often very short - one or two words, then gone. He rarely smiled, which added to his mystique; he always seemed so serious, all business, always. On the courses, he was graceful, like a cat, moving from structure to structure, rarely breaking speed. Sometimes criticized for lack of difficulty compared to some of the other competitors, he won some and lost some, relying on his speed and fluidity to win. His choice to not wear the prescribed safety suit, although adding to his danger element, was not allowed to be considered in his scoring.

"Breaking news: Latvian Aerial Athletics World Champion Ralfs Ozols has died in a fall in Shenzhen, China. Sports10 has the footage from a camera drone and warns that this footage is extremely graphic, and should only be seen by mature audiences. Ozols, who refused to wear the standard magnetic suit, risked death every time he performed, and on this fifteen-foot drop to the moving crane on your right, as you'll see, he misses the surface and goes into free fall."

The long-distance camera showed a falling Ozols, not flailing as you would expect, but instead, dropping, posed, as if at attention, arms at his side, heels together, body erect and facing forward, like a kid jumping off a train trestle into water twenty feet below, but, in this case, he was falling from over 1000 meters and rapidly accelerating as if he was a missile.

The station went to a split-screen where a close-up camera drone, one of several programmed to follow the athlete through the course, was fixed on Ozols' face. What was odd was the look on his face: he showed no expression of fear or panic, rather, he maintained his familiar, emotionless persona like one of the guards at London's Buckingham Palace.

The camera stayed fixed on his profile, capturing periodic ripples across his tight jaw, created by the increasing wind resistance.

His eyes stayed open and fixed ahead as he plummeted: twenty meters per second, then forty, then eighty. The rippling got faster and faster, as if his face was made out of crepe paper, and still, he stared ahead as he passed the 70th floor, the 60th, the 50th, without breaking form. But at about eight to ten seconds into the fall, as he was approaching a terminal velocity of over one hundred meters per second, a large tear formed, and over the next five seconds, streaked upward, toward his hairline.

Maybe it was just moisture from the abrasion of wind on his unblinking eye, or perhaps, instead, it was a tender memory, finally humanizing him in front of his audience.

The close-up camera drone pulled away as it got within fifty feet of the ground, and as the view switched to the distance camera, the streaking Ozols closed the last fifteen meters in a mere tenth of a second and jackknifed into an unrelenting concrete slab, still at attention.

After the twenty seconds of footage drew our mouths agape the announcer returned. "Ralfs Ozols was twenty-eight years old."

SKULLCRUSHER

Harold Kogler'd lived a good life, and if not for a case of mistaken identity, would probably be living one now.

Born in Austria in 1895, Harold emigrated to the States at age ten. He was a large kid who grew into a giant man. In school, Kogler excelled at strength sports, and at sixteen, and a robust six foot five inches and 360 pounds, he left school for a job in the Gransby Brother's Travelling Circus. For nine fantastic years, he traveled all over the eastern United States wowing the crowd by pressing heavy objects over his head, bending iron bars, and breaking chains.

But all that ended in 1920. As Kogler was walking downtown in Huntington, West Virginia, on a day furlough after three shows at the fairgrounds, police arrived at the scene of a bank robbery in progress. In a confusing series of events, the cops arrested Kogler as an accessory, based solely on his proximity to the crime and his appearance as, "Someone who would rob a bank if he so chose." The Gransby Brothers tried to help, hiring a local lawyer for fifty dollars but they had to leave Harold behind. "The show must go on!"

Harold, though strong of stature, was weak of mind. His attorney, a fast-speaking slickster named Willi Lundy, who had already been paid as much as he was ever going to get, convinced Harold to plead guilty for a lesser sentence. The circuit judge sentenced Harold as a bank robber to thirty years in the State Penitentiary.

Conditions at the prison were awful, and Harold, used to being on the open road and seeing nothing but happy smiling faces, sank into a deep depression. He had no idea where either his real or circus families were. The people in the Pen were nothing like a family.

Because of his size, most of the inmates left Harold alone. But one day in the yard, Moose Hawkins' gang recruited him to play basketball. Harold was familiar with the game from school, but he'd never played: he was too slow, and running tired him too easily.

He politely declined, but the diminutive Moose, who, in comparison to Harold, should have been named "Mouse," wouldn't take no for an answer. He goaded Harold, calling him a stupid palooka, a dimwit, and a sap. Harold didn't want to play, but also didn't want any trouble, so he told Moose, "Okay. I will play with ball. One time."

Moose ordered, "Just stand here by the basket, you dumb palooka, and when I give you the ball, you throw it in. Don't ever move from this spot." And to the other team Moose boasted, "Now we've got the secret weapon! You guys said he couldn't even talk. Two packs of butts for the winners."

Harold stood in his designated spot and darned if he couldn't even make one shot. Moose became more and more irritated, and, near the end of the game, losing fifteen to two, Moose kicked Harold in the knee and called timeout. Harold howled in pain as his knee buckled backwards, but he didn't go down. Instead, he took the ball from Moose, and placing it between his huge hands, he crushed it until it popped with a bang.

Moose was flabbergasted. Those who didn't like Moose applauded, in awe of Harold's strength. Moose wasn't happy when the opposing team told him that he'd forfeited and the cigarettes were theirs. He almost went after Harold, but decided to cut his losses, telling Harold in a loud voice to, "Watch your back."

Moose's gang didn't mess with Harold for a while, and he became a bit of a celebrity at the prison, though he didn't dare pop any more basketballs, which were in short supply: the one he'd popped took three months to replace.

One evening, while dining in the commons, a couple of hoodlums approached Harold from behind with homemade shivs, stabbing him in the back six times, saying, "Moose sends his regards."

Luckily for Harold, none of the stab wounds hit anything vital, and only sliced into the thick muscle on his back. The two assailants were sent to isolation as a penalty, but nothing happened to Moose. Moose continued to distance himself from Harold, but Harold knew he would never be safe from Moose's attacks. He began to eat with his back to the wall, surround himself with known supporters, and limit his activity in the yard. He sank back into a depressed state.

Moose's gang attacked Harold twice more over the following nine months, managing to slice open his cheek and neck. Harold was placed in solitary confinement "...for your own safety, 'til things cool off," but Harold felt like he was the one being penalized. In January, midway through his second year, he was re-introduced into the general population, and Moose was waiting for him.

Time had apparently made Moose bolder, and his gang was one of the most powerful in the prison. With a group of ten backers, Moose walked up to Harold in the yard and exclaimed, while beating his chest and waving his arms, "I run this yard, I run this whole fucking prison. You work for me. Got it?"

Something snapped inside Harold that day. It was not in his nature to be rash, but Moose had always managed to bring out the worst in him. He grabbed Moose by the sides of his head and headbutted him into unconsciousness, then dropped him on the concrete in front of his buddies. They were more interested in getting their boss to safety than immediate retribution, but most of them pointed and yelled at Harold, "Oh, you're gonna pay! You're dead meat, palooka! You just signed your death sentence!"

Harold saw Moose in the commons the next day, with an outlandish wrap around his head. To Harold, it looked like the one Benji the Fire-Eater used to wear at the Circus. Moose, not as amused, made gun shapes with his fingers and thumbs, pretending to shoot Harold, who was sure if someone could smuggle a gun into the Pen, it would be Moose. Three months later it was.

Moose walked across the yard with his cronies on March 16, 1922, and Harold anticipated another altercation. Moose approached, feigning geniality. "Hey there Palooka, I've been thinkin'....," and produced a snub-nosed pistol, which he fired into Harold.

Harold barely felt the bullet enter his left pectoral muscle as he lurched toward Moose, and before Moose could get another shot off, Harold had grabbed him by the coat, lifting him off the ground for another headbutt. But in an instant, realizing headbutts were temporary, his hands traded Moose's coat for his ears, and once he had a hold of Moose's head, he pressed inward.

Moose screamed as the tension in his head became unbearable, and then there was an audible crack, as the skull began to implode beneath his ears.

Harold, in a rage and seeing nothing but white, firmed his grip and pushed Moose's temples together. Both eye sockets collapsed simultaneously, one eye popping out, and the other disappearing into the skull cavity. It was at this point that someone recovered the gun and started wildly shooting at Harold, though the only thing the bullets hit was Moose, twice, in his very dead back.

Moose's head was bloody pulp, but Harold just kept pressing until his hands were only inches apart. He wailed in anguish from the physical exertion and the emotional toll of his labor, and finally gave out and slumped to the ground, his hands firmly embedded in his nemesis' skull.

Harold was treated for the gunshot wound Moose had given him, and the lacerations where bone fragments had penetrated deep into his palms. Upon release from the infirmary, he was remitted to twenty-four-hour isolation in a five by seven-foot cell.

Day after day, in the tiny cell, Harold had time to reflect on his life and how it had deteriorated into nothingness. He woke up depressed, cried to himself, and doubted he would ever get out of prison. Rumors circulated that his thirty-year sentence would be increased to life for the murder of John "Moose" Hawkins.

Time took its toll on the already mentally challenged inmate, and on a sweltering August day in 1922, on what he believed was his 27th birthday, Harold, in a fit of grief, placed his head in his hands. Apologizing to "God and everyone," with a cry of despair, he applied an effort of instantaneous pressure to his temples so violent that his skull imploded into his brain tissue.

His body was buried in an extra-large coffin in nearby Whitegate Cemetery with those of other unclaimed prisoners, two rows and eight plots down from Moose Hawkins.

EELS

I was in my thirteenth year working for Universal Salvage Limited when I joined an expedition to the western Indian Ocean. USL was, and still is to my knowledge, in the treasure-hunting business, among its more questionable import/export endeavors. Following up on a rumor or legend, we were in the Indian Ocean when a USL technician's sonar picked up a structure at a depth of around 500 feet, possibly a pirate brigantine. These large, fast, ships were one of the most desirable wrecks to locate, based on their capacity to hold shit-tons of cargo.

At the time, I was thirty-seven, a former US Navy diver by training, and had been on over twenty dive expeditions since joining USL. Some of them were fruitful, like the time we found nearly one ton of precious metals near Bermuda, and many were not. Just seaweed, rust, barnacles, and the occasional dead crewman.

This was about the farthest we had traveled to a site, although we had ventured to the South Pacific on a number of occasions. We were following the Pirate Round, a sea route starting in the European Atlantic, wrapping around the Cape of Good Hope at the tip of Africa, and up the eastern coast, past Madagascar. Seventeenth-century buccaneers would intercept trade ships from India and the Middle East as they passed through. Our particular destination was the Bulldog Bank, an area in the southern Seychelles, 500 miles outside the traditional route.

What misfortune befell our wreck remained to be seen, be it a ship-to-ship battle or just plain, old natural disaster.

The sea was remarkably clear there, due to a vast coral reef ecosystem. However, upon arriving at the dive site, we were unable to spot the wreckage from above. Even in these crystalline waters, sunlight can only penetrate so far, and we'd never been on a dive this deep where we didn't need lights no matter the clearness of the water.

We had an eight-man crew, five of us from USL, plus the boat captain and two mates. The vessel itself was run out of Seychelles, with Indian registry. It was a nice-sized craft, with a dinghy and a platform with a low freeboard allowing easy access in and out of the water.

Our closed-circuit breathing apparatuses were fitted with a Trimix air tank with a mix of oxygen, helium, and nitrogen. That setup allowed us fifteen minutes of bottom time at that depth and a four-hour (yes, four hour) re-ascent. Multiple mandatory decompression stops were required for our bodies to adjust from the high-pressure gas intake. Maybe you have heard of divers getting the "bends," a sickness where nitrogen bubbles form in the bloodstream. Consequences of rapid ascent for dives of that depth are various, many of them worse than the bends, including death.

Ben Mason was the dive leader, and though he was only thirty-one, he was one of the most experienced divers on the crew, having logged dozens of hours deep beneath the sea. The second-most experienced was my friend, Connor Berkman, and me; both of us had joined USL out of the Navy.

Five years prior, Connor and I moved into the same neighborhood, and whenever we weren't on an expedition, we were hanging out. Our wives were best friends, and our kids were best friends. Connor's son, Michael, was big into pirate ships, as I supposed the son of a fireman would be big into firetrucks. He'd made his dad a going away card with a detailed drawing of a three-mast pirate ship, with the words "Come back with the trezyur!" written beneath it.

The fourth member of our crew was Arturo Silva, who was more of an historian than a career diver, although he had been on four of the five trips before that one. And then there was the newbie, Grant Fie, who had only been diving for six years and had been with USL the past year and a half. I'd been on one dive with Grant, and he'd proved he was experienced enough to not be a danger to himself or the rest of us, so I'd personally endorsed him.

We'd reached the coordinates at about 7 a.m. and the clear blue sky and turquoise waters set the expectation for a perfect day.

We went through our preparations for the initial dive for about the tenth official time. Besides the wreck, we were not sure what we would encounter below, so the goal of the trip was to verify the presence and type of the vessel, lay claim to the site, take photos and video, and determine access points, if possible. We'd had no plans to enter the ship on this round or to remove anything from the site.

By 10 a.m., we had our tanks and equipment ready. The descent should have been quick, fifteen minutes to look around, and then, after a careful ascent, we would be back at the dive platform by 2:30.

Ben led off, dropping into the limpid waters; Grant and Arturo next, and Connor and I brought up the rear. At about sixty meters deep we started to lose much of the ambient light and had to switch on our dive lights. At about one hundred meters the ocean floor dropped off a cliff wall and faded into total darkness. The plateau above the cliff would have been a more fortunate resting spot for the wreck, but also likely one which would have caused the wreck to long ago have been picked apart by passersby.

We descended along the rocky wall for another thirty meters, and I still couldn't see the target, but at about 150 meters Ben's light bounced off a decayed mast and a barnacle-covered hull. The ship lay on its port side with the keel only about twenty feet from the bottom of the cliff, and the deck and masts pointing out toward open water. I am sure everyone's heart leapt like mine to see such an enormous vessel, a brig, undisturbed, and full of untold treasures.

We encircled the craft, Connor taking the stern and I the bow. Arturo went to work filming the ship's deck.

It was difficult to note the location of the other divers. Visibility was poor: perhaps the cliff was also casting a shadow of extra darkness over our working area. We used narrow-focused beams to penetrate the areas we were examining, and I could tell the locations of the others by seeing small dots of light that flickered in and out as they moved their inspection lights around. They were like twinkly stars, one second they'd be there, and another, gone.

After Ben secured the site with an official plaque naming USL as the claimants, he and Grant started probing the starboard hull for any possible points of entry. On ships such as these, it was often easier to access the inside through the hull than through the normal entry points off the deck.

The ship was clearly in disrepair from years in the water, but the cliff and nearby coral reefs had provided considerable protection from the violent sea and helped to preserve the overall structure. Ben and Grant methodically shone their lights in every crevice, working from the middle, outward toward Connor and me. Our jobs were to note the geography surrounding the ship to assist in the placement of potential salvage equipment. The brig itself would not be retrieved, but we use specialized machinery to harvest the cargo.

I noted curious dunes circling the base of the ship, as if it had been trapped in a giant whirlpool and dragged to the ocean floor. It is standard protocol to document the current patterns for positioning retrieval rigs on the surface, but I felt no current here. The water was awkwardly still, a sensory deprivation, with nothing tugging at my suit.

Most of the ground was rocky, but I detected a four-foot-wide swath of fine sand that hugged the cliff wall, also indicative of current, but in a place where there was none. Regardless, other than the proximity to the cliff, there were no serious retrieval concerns to be noted.

I swam around to the stern to meet up with Connor. As I rounded what used to be the quarterdeck, I focused my beam toward him, about ten yards past the ship, near the cliff wall. I scanned the area, and when I got to a spot a few feet above Connor's head, an unexpected shimmer of light reflected back.

Maybe it was a brief thought of golden doubloons spilled into the cracks of the wall, but I swam toward the glint to investigate.

I moved my beam back to the point of the reflection and once again caught a pair of shiny objects deep within a grotto. But instead of gold coins, the twinkle belonged to the eyes of two small eels that wriggled around Connor and down the length of the cliff.

I watched them disappear, and decided to re-check the alcove. The entire three-foot opening was filled with the menacing face of the largest moray eel I'd ever seen. My heart froze as I understood the bizarre tracks on the seafloor.

Though I had seen giant morays on several occasions, some as long as ten feet, none had a head larger than a man's. However, the beast, now poised in the cave above Connor, had a head easily ten times the size of my own.

Like me, the giant eel was summing up his situation, although I was certain I was the more fearful of us. I am also sure he had no idea what was behind my beam, which was why he had not yet charged me. And he couldn't, or hadn't, seen Connor directly below the grotto. However, Grant, who was completing his cycle of the side of the ship had now stopped at the stern to inspect an opening in the hull.

He was waving his beam in Connor's direction for him to check it out, and I could tell the creature in the cave, which might have been afraid of my direct light, was equally fascinated by the movement of Grant's. I had no way to audibly warn Grant or Connor that there was a veritable sea monster in the alcove above, so I directed them with my finger toward Ben.

Connor understood and started along the wall. He tried to get Grant to join him, but Grant refused, signaling he needed the last minutes of bottom time to examine the portal. Connor gave up and swam off, his light beam ultimately training directly on Ben.

At that moment the giant creature bolted from its grotto, tumbling both Grant and Connor in its wake as it moved to attack the illuminated Ben.

Now, I don't know if you have ever seen a moray eel feeding, but they have a second set of jaws way back on their skull. As they distend their jawline to engulf prey, these act as a secondary crushing force after the initial bite.

I doubt Ben had time to know what was coming by the time the super eel reached him. The eel gaped its huge jaw over Ben's head and upper torso and then crushed his tank, setting off an underwater explosion, and spooking the creature, who scaled the far side of the rock wall and disappeared past our line of sight.

Connor switched off his light, becoming invisible, at least to us; however, Grant, frozen in his spot, nervously thrust his beam in all directions.

Like Connor, I killed my light and started to back away toward the deck and beyond to the open water, but I had only moved about fifteen feet before a second enormous dark void appeared..

Grant was grabbed by his legs as the eel darted along the ground creating ripples in the sand. It scaled the side of the cliff with Grant sticking out like a cigar, except the eel was too close, and the rock wall sheared off Grant's head and torso on the jagged surface. I turned to flee, not waiting to see what else might have happened to him. I reckoned Connor had also seen the second attack and would be making his way out to open water.

As I passed the deck I spotted Arturo cowering in a small nook. Apparently, he had witnessed at least one of the two fatalities and, like the rest of us, decided it was best to hide. I signaled to him that we needed to swim away from the wreck and the cliff, and toward the open water to make our ascent. He shook his head no, as if the tiny crevice would save him from the jaws of a behemoth eel.

The timetable for the return of the eels was uncertain, but quickly firmed up as the boat rocked. Something slammed into it from the rear, which I could only guess was one of them coming back for more.

But what was even more disturbing was the shaking of the ship. Like it was alive. I realized that there were more eels inside the hull. Dozens. Or hundreds. It was then that I saw, across the deck, not thirty feet away, an open passageway to the hull. I pointed furiously at the opening and grabbed Arturo, signaling, "Now!"

Eels of all sizes started pouring out, not necessarily to attack us, but in reaction to the commotion outside. Arturo bolted for the surface, neglecting the decompression stops and setting off nitrogen bombs in his skin and organs.

I went with plan A and swam toward the open water with a pack of eels on my tail. To my right, Connor was doing the same. Surely the eels would not want to venture far from the safety of the cliff wall... but who knows what goes through the mind of demented eels when strangers invade their home?

I didn't know if the smaller eels were a real threat, but I didn't wait to find out. A good two hundred yards from the ghastly ship and it seemed the eels were gone.

But as I signaled a thumbs-up to Connor, he frantically pointed back. A second later I was punched with so much force that my tank became dislodged and fell to the bottom. I was disoriented in the dark gray water and was sure I had a broken rib. It had to be the giant eel, or eels, coming back for us. In pain, I followed my line to the tank and retrieved it, but I couldn't put it back on – my shoulder was dislocated.

I did my ascent more or less as planned, never feeling safe, even from this distance, even when I reentered the high visibility zone.

Connor was gone. I would have seen him, especially in the last fifty meters. I reflected on our friendship and mourned for him and his family as I slowly rose, until I breached the surface just after 2p.m.

The boat circled to me. They had picked up a still-alive Arturo, three hours prior, with his skin blistered over his entire body. Despite blasting him with pure oxygen, he died within minutes of being pulled from the sea.

I asked about Connor, not knowing, but knowing, that he had been taken by the eel. We waited for him on the off-chance he had drifted, but after a couple more hours scouring the ocean surface, we gave up.

—

USL compensated Connor's family generously, and they relocated to Arizona for a fresh start. Six months later, USL bombed the dive area with depth charges, and judging it safe, did another dive and discovered the only treasure was four chests of common supplies. No super eels were found, dead or alive.

I had a mild case of the bends, but a terrible case of post-traumatic stress disorder. I have not been back in the water since, even to the neighborhood pool. Most nights I dream of eels, so many eels the ocean is suffocating, choking on them. Giant eels with lightning speed, ten-inch pointy teeth, and pharyngeal jaws powerful enough to compress a metal tank. And they attack with a scream that sounds like my own.

MIRROR IMAGE

To say I'm a bit of a narcissist would be like saying Michael Jordan was a bit of a basketball player. When I was a young girl, I would take and post hundreds of selfies, living in my camera's reflection. I was crazy about my appearance, making sure my face was clean, and my hair and makeup were always perfect. I had no bad side, and all my pictures looked great.

But last year, I was in a head-on collision, and after I got out of the hospital, I couldn't stand the sight of myself in the camera. I now had a jagged, three-inch-long scar on my left cheek from where the doctors stitched me up. I could have covered it with foundation and looked the same as before, however, I felt, well, unbalanced. I also developed an irrational fear of mirrors. As much as the camera and mirrors had been a part of my life I suddenly understood the image I was looking at in them was backwards.

I'm not dumb. I mean, people who don't know me might think any girl who takes hundreds of selfies of herself every day is dumb, but I'm actually a good student. I know mirrors reflect back an image that's flipped, but, before, it never occurred to me that I was seeing myself in reverse.

Now, it was way beyond odd; it was terrifying to me that everything was the opposite of what others saw. I started to avoid the most important aspect of my life, to capture what I thought was my face, now not just imperfect, but frustratingly reversed, every time I took a photo.

Merely looking into the mirror or the camera gave me feelings of dread: knowing that what *I* was seeing was a lie, that strangers knew me better than I knew myself. I wasn't sure who I really was anymore.

So, I decided the only solution was to regain the symmetry in my face. And since I couldn't make the scar disappear, there was only one logical course of action to take.

In the mirror, I copied my scar on the opposite cheek with a fine-point Sharpie, and after careful evaluation, and three days of attempts, it was perfect. I took the X-acto knife from my stepdad's tool chest and cut through the line. There was a lot of pain, despite me first taking some of my mom's Percocet, and I was bleeding over the Sharpie ink, but I managed to get it done.

I had to cut deep enough to need stitches, not just a Band-Aid. At the hospital, my mom had to admit me because I'm still a minor, which was a little embarrassing, but not as embarrassing as having a scar on one side and not the other. It took them thirty minutes to stitch it all up, and I was hopeful that after it healed I would again be "in balance."

My stepdad, Gary, yelled at me and called me, "...a stupid, conceited bitch," but even if he was right about the "conceited" part, it wasn't necessarily stupid to heal my mind with a little physical discomfort. And I reasoned that once I was in balance again, I could easily cover up the scars with makeup and resume my normal life.

Unfortunately, after the stitches were removed, I was not at all happy with the result. The shadows off the raised scar were different, and the new right scar was about an eighth of an inch lower on my face than the original one. It had to be corrected. Gary hid all the X-acto knives (not that I blamed him), but I found a box cutter. I cut a little above the right scar and a little below the left scar to make sure they were the same height, and after it stopped bleeding, I verified it with a ruler, and I was satisfied.

Also, I didn't think I needed stitches. I went deep, but very short, and the cuts didn't bleed much, so I just avoided my mom and Gary for a few days. But after day three the cuts started to look like they weren't healing well, and by day four both were discolored. I panicked, and after frantically searching the internet, I concluded I hadn't sterilized the box cutter, and the incisions were probably infected.

Luckily for me, they had given me a tetanus shot after my first attempt, but I needed antibiotics, which Mom had (she's a walking drugstore). The wounds were swollen, oozing pus, and didn't look like they would ever heal. And one was at the top of one scar and the other at the bottom of the other, so now I was even further out of balance. While those were healing, I used some sandpaper to file away the raised skin of the second scar. I did this on both sides, and the redness helped to blur the scar lines a bit, but I looked windburned.

I should probably mention that my right eye started twitching above the box cutter incision. I thought I might have hit a nerve. This was pretty unsettling, and it got worse over the next week.

I took some muscle relaxers (not Mom's, actually Gary's), which seemed to help, but I figured that was only a short-term solution. I asked my friend Amy if it was noticeable, and after a lengthy explanation of why I had new, infected cuts all over my face, she said she couldn't see my eye twitching. I think I yelled at her, "I'm not a liar!" When I calmed down, I decided I needed a professional opinion.

Now, obviously, my mom is no stranger to the doctor. She's what's referred to as a "frequent flyer." She told me it was probably not nerve damage, just stress. She gave me some Xanax, and after looking up the symptoms on the computer, I think she was right. There's a condition called ocular myokymia, which can affect only one eye and be related to stress.

After three weeks of taking the Xanax, the eye-twitching was gone, but I wanted to start using them twice a day, and I was running out. A sketchy guy in my chem class pointed me toward this other sketchy guy, Derek, who "might sell drugs" behind the gym.

When I asked Derek if he knew anyone with Xanax, he said he could hook me up with "Benzos" – benzodiazepines. He said I should try Valium because it was better than Xanax for muscle spasms. So now I had a dealer. I got fifty of them, which I thought was a reasonable amount, for only $150, and they worked great. Unfortunately, there were a couple of minor side effects and a couple of major ones.

One minor side effect was that I was high all the time: at school, at the dinner table, even while sleeping. My grades were dropping, after several missed assignments, and I didn't really care. I stopped worrying so much about my complexion, and thought, *it is what it is*.

A major side effect was that I now had a growing drug habit, and I began experimenting with other drugs, fairly innocuous things like pot, and some bigger ticket items like K-pin (like Valium, but better) and Oxy. I also started drinking vodka Red Bulls, and also vodka without Red Bull. I would get confused about what I had taken and when.

One Saturday night I headed over to Amy's house and rolled my car off the side of a bridge. This time I was pinned in the car and the lower half of my right leg had to be amputated.

I'm in two rehabs, for my leg and for my drug addiction, but I think I'm going to be okay. I haven't seriously thought about cutting off my other leg. I haven't.

FLAT ANN

"He treats me good; you know?"

Ann's response to Emily's concerned question did not hit the reassuring tone she was seeking.

"But, Annie, I'm worried about you. He's got a reputation of you know... being into bad stuff.... And he's married. How's that gonna turn out for you?"

"I dunno. Maybe he'll leave her for me. You know..., he's loaded."

"Yeah, loaded with bullets. I don't trust him, Annie. You deserve better."

Emily and Ann, best friends since Catholic school in Bensonhurst, were having the same discussion they'd had every week for the past three months, ever since Ann showed up with bruises around her lips courtesy of one Mr. Francis "Frank" Conti, an up-and-coming "businessman" in their largely Italian neighborhood. Ann had been his "best girl," or rather one of them, from the first time she set foot in the Costa Club, a velvety speakeasy run by Frank.

She was a clever woman: grew up doing the books for her father's chain of Five and Dimes. But Frank wasn't interested in her smarts; he was more after her inordinately large set of hooters that protruded from her curvy frame. To his associates, he referred to her as "Fat Ann, the One with the Big Bazookas," using all eight words, every time he mentioned her, so reliably that his subordinates would mouth the last six words to themselves each time.

It was their third date when Frank smacked her. Ann had suggested that maybe Mr. Conti needed an upgrade from Mrs. Conti, and she, Ann, might be the one. Frank was quick to put Ann in her place. "Don't evah disrespect me or my wife again!" Ann thought this was ironic because they'd gone all the way on date number two.

Frank gave her a righteous backhand that drew blood, and Ann, not backing down, told him, "You'll miss these," and heaved up her big gals for him to see. Frank dismissed her, but she was right: he called her to the Costa Club two days later.

Ann was around Frank enough to know he was up to no good, but she was drawn to bad boys. She had previously dated several nefarious teens in the neighborhood, but they were just kids. Frank and Mrs. Conti had the life she wanted: cars and money and jewelry and power, and despite Emily's best efforts to turn her friend to the straight and narrow, Ann decided to go all-in on Frank, threatening to expose his operation to the cops if he didn't leave his wife.

Frank was not one to deal with such ultimatums. He shot Ann in the stomach, just so she had time for his final lecture on "The one and only, Mrs. Conti," before administering a second shot between her eyes.

Frank's underlings, a ridiculous bumbling pair from his old neighborhood nicknamed Jimmy Peashooter and Donny the Catfish, heard the shots and knocked on the door to Frank's office. "Boss, you okay in there?"

"Yes, you two dimwits, get in here and clean up this mess."

"Ooooh," said Jimmy P, "she's dead," overstating the obvious, as the blood pool rapidly spread around Ann's head.

"Get rid of her," ordered Frank. Then, "Naw, don't just get rid of her. I want you guys to flatten her out. Run her over and over until she's thin, like a pancake."

"But, Boss," exclaimed Donny, the C, "she's already dead; we should just throw her in the rivva."

"*Did you hear me*? Flat! Flat as a Pancake!"

"Okay boss," and the two lackeys struggled to haul the robust Ann out the door and into the back of the car. They drove out to the woods on Long Island, where they had a secret remote spot to do the deed.

Jimmy wondered aloud, "So, whut? Just puttah on the ground? And then runnah ovah a few times?"

Donny, whose IQ was a few points higher, replied, "You heard the boss: *flat*. We gotta run her ovah 'n ovah, and then we'll puttah in a shallow grave. Real shallow, if you know what I mean. Heh heh."

"Yeah, real shallow, Donny. Heh heh."

So they ran over Ann with the car, but she was quite substantial, and there were some trouble areas, particularly her thick bones and hardy skull. However, her enormous bosom was no longer, and Donny quipped, "No more Fat Ann; now she's *flat* Ann! Heh heh," pleased with his joke. When Jimmy P. didn't realize that it was a play on, "Fat Ann," Donny explained, "Ya know; she was Fat Ann? Now she's *f-l-a-t* Ann."

And Jimmy knew something was funny about that, so he repeated, "Yeah, Donny, Flat Ann," but still didn't really get the reference.

They dropped Anne into a remarkably shallow grave.

The next day, they stopped by Aldo's Ristorante as scheduled, to update Frank. They found Frank in the kitchen marveling at his new pasta machine. Frank inquired, "So... you two dimwits do it? How flat she get?"

"Real flat boss," Jimmy chuckled.

"Oh yeah? And her skull? Like a pancake?"

Before Donny could speak up, Jimmy P, responded, "Well, no boss, it wouldn't crush under the car, and, well, everything else was real flat." Donny winced, sensing anger before it came.

"*I said flat*! *Flat is flat*!" And he grabbed Jimmy by the wrist, feeding his fingers into the powerful pasta machine. Jimmy screamed as his fingers were crushed to bits by the rollers.

"*Flat – like this*" and he pulled the flattened digits from the roller, flopping them in front of the two stooges. Jimmy P. was still screaming his head off as Donny dragged him out of the restaurant and to the clinic on Dowry Street to get bandaged up.

"You know, Jimmy, next time you just say, 'Yes, boss, flat as a pancake.' That's what he wants, so you gotta tell him that."

Jimmy, with a sour look on his face said, "So whadda we do now?"

"Well, I think we's gotta rent one of them steamrollahs: the ones with the big heavy wheel on da front that they use to make da roads? And den we gotta go dig her up. And den we gotta drive dat over her until she's flat, like the boss says."

"Good plan, Donny. I'm glad you're so smart."

So that's what the boys did. They got a steamroller from Uncle Rossi and drove back Ann's body from the woods to the abandoned lot on Third and Wilkes, and at three o'clock in the morning, they steamrolled Ann until she was level with the lot surface. They shoveled wet concrete over her and left her in that state.

Reporting to the restaurant the next day, they were sure they had atoned for their earlier mistakes.

"So," Frank started, "did you two nincompoops do as I asked? Is she as flat as ol' Jimmy's fingers? Heh heh heh...."

"Yes, boss," Donny spoke up this time. "We ran her over real good with Uncle Rossi's steamrollah. She didn't even stick up above the ground when we was trew wit her."

"So then what did you do with her?"

"We poured concrete ovah her."

"Well, I got special plans for that one. I need you guys to put her in this crate." And with that, Frank brought out a thin crate with no more than an inch between the top and bottom panels. "Boys, this was used to store maps. Put 'er in here and take her out to my junkyard; you know, the one in Jersey? I'll meet you there tomorrah, eight in da mornin'."

"Sure thing, boss," Donny agreed, while Jimmy eyed the pasta machine with hatred.

That night, Donny and Jimmy returned to the now non-abandoned lot, and with great effort, removed the concrete covering Ann's body. But as they lifted her body out of the ground, they were horrified to see that her skull and bones were still intact – they had only been pressed into the lot, where now there was a full-figured bas-relief of Ann apparent in the soil. Ann was not flat, rather, still fat. There was no way that Anne was going to fit in the one-inch-high box.

Panicked, they drove Ann to Bianchi's Garage. Donny put her head in a vise and using a crowbar on the crank, got enough leverage to crush it, and Ann's formerly-clever brain oozed out of both sides of the vise in a most disgusting manner, which made Jimmy P. regurgitate his meatloaf dinner. Piece by piece, bones were pressed in like manner, the largest, milled lengthwise into inch-high planes, and by daybreak, everything fit into the thin box, more or less.

They pulled up at the junkyard, right at eight, and Frank was waiting. He looked at the overstuffed box and back at his two henchmen, shaking his head. "Still too fat. This is my fault. I should never send boys to do a man's work."

And with that, he dismissed the boys. He might kill them later, but for now, he was content to load Ann into the car crusher and flatten her down to a half-inch, wooden map crate included.

LEVITAR

People, people, gather 'round. I stand before you to attest and atone. The Japanese legend of the Levitar is real. I have personally experienced and survived an encounter. I also have reason to believe my friend Suji-san met his demise at the hand of such a creature. You should know this, for your own selves, for your children.

Suji-san and I were always up to no good, ever since I can remember. Maybe we were rebelling against our strict parents, or maybe sometimes people are just predisposed to mischief. We would steal small treats from the neighborhood konbi or fill balloons with paint and throw them down on the cars driving under the bridges in our prefecture.

When we got older we did more mean stuff and hung out with a bad crowd. We found our way into the local yakuza by age fifteen, and started extorting businesses for protection – from us.

Only three years later, Suji-san was eating at the food court in the mall when he choked on his onigiri. But Mako-san, who was there, said it was a really strange occurrence. He said Suji-san was just eating and joking around, and then he got really serious and was looking up in the air, horrified. There was nothing there, but he could see something. Then he started choking.

Mako-san tried to get help, but people didn't want to help him because he had tattoos all over his body and his neck. Mako-san gave Suji-san the Heimlich, but then the cops were coming so he ran – he was already being monitored by the police and didn't want to be involved.

Suji-san could not be resuscitated, and he died there at the food court. Mikiyoko-san, who was the head of our yakuza, said Suji-san might have seen the Levitar right before he died. He told us the story of how the Levitar preys upon the wicked, and said that it's a known hazard of being a gangster. So we'd better watch out. And then he laughed at us like we were all baka and told us to get back to work.

After hearing the story, Mako-san pulled me aside and told me he remembered a baby laughing with his parents across the food court from them. He noticed it because the baby was exceptionally cute and happy. He said that maybe it was the Levitar..., and then he poked me and laughed like he was kidding, but I could tell he was still a little disturbed.

I moved up in the organization, and around my twenty-fifth birthday I was tasked with the kidnapping of a high-ranking official's daughter. Things went wrong, and we ended up having to kill the girl. I didn't do it personally, but I gave the order.

Only a week later, I was at a restaurant and I saw a cute baby a few tables away. It was laughing and smiling at me like a baby Budha. The parents were playing with him and I'd glance over from time to time. But once, when I looked up, he flew out of his highchair, about six feet above all the tables, and paused in front of where I was sitting. I remembered the story of the Levitar so I stopped eating to make sure I did not choke. But then the baby floated closer and closer.

I was paralyzed. I wanted to get away, but I was so fascinated by the floating baby that I did not move.

The baby was now above my table, looking down at me with eyes that pierced my soul. He opened his mouth and fire roared out and all around me. I put my hands up to guard my face and felt the hairs on my arms singe. I fell backward in my chair and onto the floor of the table behind me. I lost my paralysis, got up, and ran out the door without paying.

Every night thereafter, the Levitar visited me in my dreams: horrific, vivid dreams where I felt both paralyzed by the Levitar's dark, lifeless eyes, and then burned alive by the flames coming from his mouth.

I'd run to the shower to cool down, feeling the sting of third-degree burns, though my skin was clear. I took that as a warning to stop my criminal behavior.

My yakuza graciously let me leave. But the nightmares did not stop. Even as I changed my ways and became kind, I continue to be haunted. I try to not sleep, but still, I am overcome by daydreams and false visions. I am living a hell on earth.

So now, in front of all of you, I take this blade, the instrument of countless misdeeds, and pierce myself... release my soul... from this... dishonorable life.

Steer clear of the dark path... lest you too... encounter the... Levitar.

HEATWAVE

"I bet the people in Hell also want ice water."

Randy and I chuckled at the disconnected response to, "It's a hot one."

Normally people say that phrase to describe an unattainable wish, like, "I want a new truck."

"Oh? And people in Hell also want ice water." But ol' Dwayne would say it anytime for any reason and we never corrected him.

As usual, we were commiserating on another triple-digit day, and, somehow, the rather lame banter always provided a temporary relief.

I went over to the cooler and got out another icy rag and squeezed it over my bald head and my burning neck (we were all true rednecks in that sense). I replaced my hat, put on my work gloves, and started tearing out more broke slats on the west fence.

This project was supposed to take about eight days with just the three of us, but we were already on day eight and had about 800 yards of fence line still left to repair.

We were pretty efficient at this point, with me handling the demo; Randy doing the install, and Dwayne giving the new slats a coat of paint, but we underestimated how much work was needed. The exposure to the sun in all but the mesquite patch had taken its toll on daddy's twenty-five-year-old fence. We didn't share a border with nobody else either, other than government land, so it was just ours to maintain.

And we also underestimated how hot this bitch could get. The extra humidity had us soaked through our clothes, and we couldn't do more than about an hour at a time without risking heat exhaustion. Starting at sun-up, when it was coolest, we managed about 400 feet of fence done a day.

I figured we still had about two or three days left. I called work and told them I'd be back by Wednesday, Thursday at the latest.

Randy and Dwayne didn't care; I was paying them by the day, but for me, I had to return to my regular job in Austin. This was just a passion, keeping up daddy's ranch. But I was happy to blow most of my saved-up vacation to cook out here, only forty miles from the Mexican border. In a few years I'd retire out here and count the stars, away from the haze and noise of the city.

We headed back to the cabin at noon, to get some lunch and a brief break from the relentless heat. Dwayne was on the couch and said he didn't feel so good. We gave him some shit about pussin' out on us for the rest of the day, but he said he was dizzy like he was gonna pass out. I thought maybe he had some mild heat exhaustion, so we told him to chill out, and we'd keep working on the fence. He could catch up with us when he felt better.

Randy and I went back out to the field around 1:30 and worked 'til about 6. We were burning up and agreed Dwayne probably had the right idea to sit the afternoon out. But, when we got back to the cabin, Dwayne was lying on the floor deader than a doornail. I tried to revive him, but it was no use. Randy went outside and puked all over the front steps. He and Dwayne had been friends for sixty years.

We tried to call 911, but there was no cell tower near enough to get through. After he'd settled down, Randy said he'd go out for help. All the way to Uvalde if he had to. I agreed, and Randy took the truck.

It wasn't but thirty minutes later that the power went out. It was always going out down here: people overloading the grid, using their AC and what not. I hoped it wouldn't be long, and the power'd be back up again shortly. Randy'd be back with the truck and help for Dwayne, and then we could go into town to spend the night if we had to.

But Randy didn't come back, the police and ambulance never arrived, and the power remained off. I was stranded in the cabin with no electricity and my dead friend in the den. I tried calling Randy several times, but the signal was never strong enough. Once I had a bar, but by the time it rang through it had gone back to zero.

It was close to midnight, six hours gone by, and I feared the worst: Randy had gotten himself into some type of accident.

Best thing for me would be to sit tight. The cabin was still cooler than outside, and I knew I could keep poor Dwayne company.

I woke up at 5 a.m, drenched in sweat. The cabin was hot as hell. Luckily, I had ice water, or cold enough water anyway. Daddy had a dug deep well on the property. I drank quite a bit of it and raised a glass in memory of Dwayne: he was a good man and definitely in heaven, not hell, probably with a cold one in his hand.

I checked my phone for messages from Randy, and it was on one percent battery. I found Dwayne's phone, which still had about twenty percent. Also no service, but better than nothing.

Needless to say, fence-building was indefinitely suspended. Stay inside, stay hydrated, and wait for help were on the agenda. This was Monday, and no one came.

That night, I took Dwayne's phone and headed out toward town to try to get a signal. It was almost drained. I should've turned it off earlier. Out in the sticks where we were, the phones are constantly searching for signal, which runs down the battery extra fast. I figured I had a couple of hours, max.

It was still hot, even after sundown. This area ain't like the desert; it stays hot all night. I should have gone out at 4 a.m. when it was the coolest. There's also all sorts of critters out at night, and coyotes. I had my gun, but I didn't know if I could fend off a pack of coyotes.

I walked to the edge of the property, which was about two miles, then kept walking about another hour and got a signal. I dialed, and the operator got out, "911 what's your—" before the phone died. I was hopeful it was enough of a connection that they'd find me. I sat tight along the road enjoying the night air, but loathing the sound of the cicadas. I hate them things. No one came, and after a couple of hours, I headed back toward the house.

Dwayne was starting to ripen up. Walking in after being out for a while attuned me to the stench. I made a cocoon for him with some sheets to try to curtain the odor, and, by the time I was done, I was satisfied it had worked.

We still had no power, but the cabin's shower water was cool. I considered storing Dwayne in the bathtub, but I needed to keep that for myself.

Tuesday came and went, and nobody stopped by. I knew it'd be Thursday or Friday before I was missed at work. I shouldn't have told them "Wednesday or Thursday at the latest," because it sounded open-ended. My friend Chuck knew where I was, but other than that, I had no family. Neither did Dwayne or Randy, although Randy had an on-again-off-again relationship with his landlord.

Speaking of Randy, I feared he had also died. It was the only logical explanation for why he hadn't returned. So, desperate to avoid the same fate as my friends, I started the fire.

We had all this discarded wood from the fence piled up by the house. I figured I could get a good bonfire going, and maybe someone would see the smoke and come.

At dusk, I began to drag planks about a hundred yards upwind from the cabin. The distance was enough to keep the cabin safe, even if the wind shifted, and it was close enough I could personally haul an amount of wood to create a significant burn pile. I moved most of the boards by morning, then lit that sucker up. It was nice and smoky.

Coming back in from the job, I noticed. *Wow, Dwayne was really rank.* I suppressed a gag and went straight back outside into the heat.

I had to get him out of there ASAP, even though I was sure the odor had permanently tainted the cabin. Earlier, when I woke up, it wasn't even noticeable, but it had become like rotten meat mixed with puss.

I told Dwayne I was sorry, but he was going to have to sleep outside from now on. I dragged his bloated 230-pound body down the porch steps and across to the tool shed. I debated about putting him in the shed or leaving him outside, but I didn't want him to be eaten by coyotes, so, reluctantly, I put him in inside. Turned out to be the right move as the coyotes came calling that night, and try as they might, they didn't get into that shed.

The bonfire plan failed to generate traffic to the cabin, but I tried again and again, and kept that fire burning best I could. I was able to maintain my temperature with the showers, but was running out of food and had no energy to hunt. That's when I got hunted.

I was in the bedroom, napping around dusk, when I heard a tap-tap-tap on the wooden floor in the living room. I thought maybe I was being saved, but then I saw a low shape comin' through the doorway, and knew coyotes were in the house. I started firing the shotgun at them, but they kept coming, like zombies. You'd think they be like, "Naw, this ain't for me," and run back out. But two got in during my reload, and I had to hit 'em with the butt and scramble out the door.

That's when the siren tweeted and the cruiser pulled up, thank God.

They told me to drop the gun (for their own protection, of course), and explained they were doing a wellness check throughout the areas that lost power. They hadn't seen the smoke until after they were on the property and didn't think anything of it anyway. People burn stuff all the time out in these parts.

The deputy phoned for an ambulance. I thought I was alright but the deputy didn't think so. Neither did the EMTs, who strapped me to a gurney and took me to the medical center. They said I was experiencing heatstroke. Apparently, I had started pulling apart daddy's cabin, including the front and back doors, to keep the fire burning. I thanked them for takin' care of the coyotes, but they said they didn't see any. I must have hallucinated that.

They found Dwayne in the shed and believed my story about him being dead from the heat. They also informed me that Randy had a one-man collision with a telephone pole about ten miles from the ranch, only about a quarter mile from where I had called 911. He had been airlifted to San Antonio and was in an induced coma.

I was on a medical leave of absence for a week, but fine after that. Randy came out of his coma. He didn't remember the accident or driving from the cabin, but otherwise, he was okay. We had a funeral for Dwayne, and we buried him in the grove near Daddy and Momma, in the northwest corner of the ranch.

I hired a few day laborers to finish the fence and rebuild the cabin, and we even got Dwayne's smell out of there.

I finally did retire out here all alone, but now I've got a regular doomsday setup: two generators, an ATV, extra gas, and satellite internet. Nothing like that's ever gonna happen to me or my friends out at daddy's property again. Randy still visits me from time to time, as a guest, not a worker, to pay his respects to Dwayne.

And we drink ice water, and we count the stars, and we count our blessings.

Author's Note:

In the fall of 2006, my sister and I were cleaning out my dad's study shortly after he died. We found a leatherbound journal, roughly the size of a paperback novel, in a side desk drawer. The journal contained hundreds of very thin pages, each of which had been meticulously penned by hand.

An inscription on the first page identified the owner as Sir William Burroughs, who I found to be my great, great, great grandfather. Leafing through the pages, I could tell it was a memoir of his travels, with dates from the early 1800's and tales recounting his experiences in exotic places like India, Hong Kong, and Africa.

A red ribbon, which I initially assumed was placed randomly placed in the middle of the book, was at the start of a section called "Ngachu." I now don't think its placement was random.

The below is a direct transcription from that section.

It was my first and last time to visit Ngachu. The four-day journey from the outpost was arduous, through dense foliage and treacherous vines, on foot to the middle of the forest. The pygmies, who villaged near the outpost, warned against the expedition, saying it was, "No good," and, "cursed," when referring to the deserted location thirteen miles to the southeast. Our colleagues, Brighton and Thompson, had disappeared on a similar expedition only nine months prior, so the danger was palatable.

Our guides, who feared lasting effects from the visit, agreed to take us only as a far as the first clearing, a spot no more than the size of a small bedroom in a London flat. We were given precise directions on how to proceed, and they returned to the outpost, leaving us to continue our journey alone.

The three of us camped in the clearing overnight, rather than risk becoming disoriented in the growing dusk. Even in the middle of the day the canopy of trees muted the vibrant foliage to grey. Though we had seen no wildlife, we made a fire for protection against a possible predator. Unencumbered by the irrational fears of the pygmy guides, we slept soundly and awoke to enjoy a carafe of warm coffee over the dying embers of the fire.

Middleton and Smith brandished machetes and started to cleave their way into the vegetation, using the methods we had learnt over the prior days. It was expected to only be about 200 yards to Ngachu, but after four hours it seemed we were only a quarter of the way. I got my hands dirty helping, and, just at nightfall, we found the enclave: ten rotting mud and leaf huts around a central pit of stones. We could see clear through to the sky, which emptied its contents on us as we scrambled to the closest hut for refuge.

As we burst through the opening, a man sitting on a chair stared back at me, and I lost my nerves. I am not too proud to say I screeched at the sight of him. Middleton was right behind me, and I heard him mutter, "Oh my," over the sound of my own heartbeat. We knew the man was no longer alive, but in the dim light it was difficult to tell how long he had been deceased.

Smith entered and was startled, as Middleton and I had been a moment before. But he walked over and stood close to the man.

"Remarkable," he said calmly. "Real skin, taxidermy. And the eyes... the eyes are polished stone. Onyx? or... black diamond?"

The dead man was dressed in ceremonial clothing, and his skin was weathered, as if it had been tanned, like hide. Though it was unnerving to be in the presence of the former chieftain, the shelter provided modest relief from the downpour, imperfect everywhere other than above the deceased man, where the roof had been reinforced with layers of thatching, protecting him from the deluges that were frequent in this part of the country.

As my eyes adjusted to the dim light, and as my resolve took effect—because I realized that I was likely spending the night in this hut—I managed to tolerate our fourth companion as he sat, unslouching, at attention, at the edge of the round room. I did not detect an odour coming from him, and other than Smith commenting on the man's real skin, he might as well have been a wax likeness vis-à-vis those at Madame Tussaud's back home.

We were curious about the other huts and the potential for archaeological treasure but decided to wait until morning, expecting the rain to subside by then. We blocked the door the best we could by laying our gear across the opening and settled in for the night.

I nicknamed the Chief "Punch," after the puppet. He had a striking resemblance, although he was determinedly more serious. He was also a diminutive man, no more than four feet and six inches, even smaller than the average pygmy males near the outpost. It might have been his size that was most unnerving as he sat there and stared at the door like a doll from some horror story that comes alive in the middle of the night to slay the family.

Despite our exhaustion from the physical effort of penetrating the thick jungle, we were wide awake. Perhaps we wanted to keep an eye on Punch, or possibly our excitement was counteracting the fatigue. We had some bread with a quaff of gin, and tonic laced with quinine to fight off malaria, and finally drifted off to sleep.

At daybreak, I ventured out to relieve myself, but waited for Middleton and Smith before investigating the other huts. The central pit had drained, and the ground was not as muddy as I would have thought with such a fierce rain. I deduced we were on a small hill, and the water ran off all around the clearing. I re-entered the hut and Smith was poking at the side of the Chief.

"He's stuffed with some material, and light as a feather. He has a proper stick up his arse to keep him upright and attached to the chair, and together they are no more than three stone."

I laughed at poor Punch, picturing him performing at a giant puppet show on the end of a proper stick. I commanded the team to start working our way around the small village clockwise.

Inside the next hut were old cooking tools made of iron and several pairs of shackles. Clearly, these were not obtained in the forest nor available in the surrounding villages. And while an iron poker, or knife, or shovel, might have been introduced by travellers, the shackles were definitely out of place.

We noticed dried blood halfway up the poker, and on the shovel and knives, but what was more disturbing was dried blood on the shackles. We deduced there was some butchering of live animals, but who would shackle a pig? We believed it was human blood on all of the instruments.

In the third hut we found a family of four, but instead of being attached to the chair as the Chief was, they were propped at the compass points of the room. An older man, a woman, and two boys, all of them were naked. Each of them had their real skin and were stuffed like the Chief. It was odd that no scavengers had ever ventured onto the site; the bodies were undisturbed. They appeared to be sleeping, with their eyes sewed shut, the precious gemstone eyes reserved for the Chief only.

The smallest boy was no more than six years old, judging by his teeth. The Chief and three of the people in the second hut had their mouths sewed shut, but the young boy's mouth was agape. It had never been sewn. But it didn't look ghastly as you would expect. It was more as if he was singing and the others were simply listening. I was familiar with some of the pygmy songs from my time visiting this general area before, and I could almost hear the tune in my head.

We spent considerable time in each hut measuring and sketching the contents. By noon, we had visited five huts, including the original. Other than the hut with the tools, each of the other dwellings had residents, stuffed and posed. We hoped to make it through the other seven huts by nightfall. Our rations were sufficient to stay an extra day, but our guides were expecting us, so we had no choice but to accelerate our studies.

Since the hut at the end of the settlement was twice the size of the others, we expected it would take some time. We broke for a lunch of bread and water and a bit of canned meat, which was a mistake, because in the sixth hut, furthest from the Chief's, we made our most gruesome discovery.

The door to the sixth hut did not face the central courtyard, but rather the jungle. As we circled the structure, I became uneasy as I felt the jungle's eyes upon me. There was also an odour coming from the hut. Upon entering I promptly turned around and vomited at the edge of the tree line.

So many bodies were piled up in that sixth hut. Forty-two as we later counted. They were all eviscerated, but the skulls and hides were in various stages of preparation. It was like being in a dollmaker's workshop, with piles of straw in between the flattened hides and the piles of stuffed bodies. None of the entrails or bones of the bodies were evident.

There were two great vats of an oily solution in the corner of the hut. In the solution were chunks of matter which appeared to be brains. Smith retrieved a shoot from the forest and pulled out a rather large piece of flesh, which confirmed our assessment. This was the tanning solution.

The sense of disgust was only replaced by a sense of dread that the work was ongoing, and that we were in danger. A rustle in the trees startled me, but it was only a thrush. I didn't like the exit pointing out to the jungle, so I told the others I was going back to the Chief's lodge for air. This is when Middleton said, "Oh my god, white people."

Sure enough, near the bottom of the pile of unstuffed bodies were the ample and pallid frames of two Anglo-Saxon males. Could it have been Brighton and Thompson?

Given this new development, I reasoned that this was not solely a tribal custom, but was the preparation for the dead. And the bodies were recent.

I told the others my theory, and though they heartily agreed, they decided to continue cataloguing while I took a break. I walked back to the Chief's hut, taking a moment for a peek inside the remaining huts on the right side of the courtyard. All of the huts were ordinary, like the first five, although one might argue that stuffed and posed bodies were anything but ordinary.

While reviewing my notes I heard one of my companions cry out. It was only for a second, but I rushed outside to find out what had gone wrong. In the centre of the courtyard, facing the sixth hut, was a pigmy leader and two attendants. Smith, whose throat was slit, was being dragged to the courtyard and Middleton behind him. Both were dead.

The natives were struggling with the large men, easily twelve to fourteen stone each, and no one had spotted me. I crept backwards into the hut with the Chief, grabbed my satchel, inserted my notebook, and withdrew my revolver, a three-shot pepperbox mainly used for defence against wild animals.

I was certain that if I stayed in the hut, I would be trapped and killed, so I headed out into the open with my gun pointed at the chief. One of the natives charged me, and I fired, knocking him to the ground, presumably dead. The rest of the tribe began to charge, and then the leader shouted for them to stop. I aimed straight at the leader and backed toward the path we had cleaved through the forest. It was clear the leader did not know that I only had two shots left. I motioned for them to back up, pointing the revolver back and forth between the leader and whichever tribesman was closest.

The leader dropped to his knees and bowed before me. The other tribesmen followed suit, dropping Smith and Middleton into the mud facedown as they also got to their knees. I desperately wanted to avenge my colleagues, or slowly back into the forest and flee, but either of these tactics would have likely stirred the tribe into action. So, continuing to train my revolver on the leader, I moved toward the second hut and grabbed the shackles.

I threw them at the leader and signalled for the man at his right to assist. The leader put out his hands and feet and let his man apply the shackles.

I forced all eleven tribesmen into the shallow pit. One started yelling and trying to incite a riot, and I shot my firearm over their heads, which worked to silence him. I went just inside the first hut and reloaded my weapon there so they would not see how time-consuming it was. I also grabbed Smith's revolver. Middleton had a flintlock, which was impractical for me to carry, so I hid it behind the Chief.

The tribesmen were still sitting in the pit, now with two weapons pointed at them. They trembled in fear, and I almost felt sorry for them, then glanced at Smith and Middleton and my rage returned. I added twenty times the normal dosage of quinine powder to each of two tonic flasks which I threw into the pit. I drank from my own flask, and all but the leader followed suit.

I planned to escape long before darkness, when surely the tribe would have an advantage. Waiting for the quinine to take effect was my only plan, and I feared these men may have had an immunity, when suddenly, and spectacularly, they started to double over in pain and retch as the toxin took over their bodies. The leader, understanding the water had been tainted, commanded his tribesmen to attack, but by now they were feeble and disoriented, enabling me to pick them off one by one with the rifle and the two handguns.

Then it was only me and the tribal leader. He remained in the centre of the pit, slain tribesmen all around, while I walked to the sixth hut. Grabbing a handful of straw I came upon him and forced the straw into his mouth, holding his nose shut and suffocating him as punishment for the deaths of my colleagues. I left him dead in the pit with a mouthful of straw and fled into the forest. The path back to basecamp was navigable, and I made it just after nightfall, recounting my struggle to the rest of our party.

Three months later, upon my recommendation, the pygmy camp at Ngachu was invaded by British authorities. The bodies of Smith, Middleton, Brighton, and Thompson were retrieved for a proper burial, and I was told the whole of the village was burned for sanitary reasons: the huts, the invaders, Punch, the singing boy, and the denizens of Ngachu, stuffed and unstuffed. I continued my travels in central Africa for ten more years, and never had such a harrowing experience again.

There are days when I wake up in this flat and want to bolt out the door, back to Ngachu to verify there are no remnants of that haunted place. But I've come to realize that as long as I can sit here at this very desk and recall the odours of straw and tanning solution and the blood of so many men, Ngachu still lives on inside me.

MEGAN, SIDESADDLE

Doctor, I'm struggling with a very troubling image of my daughter, Megan. She died last year when she was six when she slipped on a mossy rock at the lake and hit her head. I was coping, but since about three weeks ago, I started seeing her sitting on the hood of our car whenever we are driving. I know she can't be there, but it seems very real to me. She's sitting sidesaddle, with her feet off the side of the hood and she's balancing on the edge without anything to keep her on. I'm afraid she's going to fall off and I can't bear the thought of that.

I have a good idea where this is coming from. When I travel to China for work, I often see small children, even toddlers, in traffic, on the back of mopeds, where'd you'd tie up schoolbooks. They just sit there, with no seatbelts, and I always think they're going to fall off and be killed. Maybe for normal children this is no big deal, but Megan suffered from benign paroxysmal vertigo. She'd get dizzy and lose balance all of a sudden. We think this is what happened on the rocks.

The first time I saw her was when Thom picked me up from the airport. I had just come back from three weeks in Shanghai. I looked out my front window and saw Megan sitting there on the hood, with her feet dangling over the side, in her favorite red dress with white flowers, and without a care in the world. Though I knew she wasn't really there, I told Thom to slow down. I was so concerned for her safety, even though she clearly wasn't real. I wouldn't take my eyes off her until we stopped. As we pulled into our driveway, she disappeared, and I started crying in confusion of what had just happened.

It's like when you put your coffee cup on top of the car, and you forget, and you drive off, and it goes everywhere. It's like we had put her up there while we were getting in the car and forgot. That's an extreme example; of course we'd never leave one of our children on top of a car, but maybe she's telling us we should have paid more attention when she wandered down to the lakeline.

Last Sunday we went to the farmer's market, over off County Road 415. And part of that road is very bad, and she was vibrating so much I just knew she'd be bumped off. Madison asked me why I was crying, and I just told her that I missed Megan, but that wasn't really it; it was like I was going to lose her again.

It's been hard on Thom and Madison, and they'd understand if I still missed my little girl, but Thom doesn't understand this. I don't understand this.

When she's on the hood, I can see her so clearly, it's like she's really alive. And she's so happy, the way I want to remember her. A part of me wants to keep seeing her, but I'm sure that's an unhealthy response to grief, and it's not fair to my family.

So, I guess, what I'm asking, doctor, is… should I let her fall off?

URANIUM MINE

"They're coming! They're coming!" Eliab, a lookout, ran over the northern hill toward our encampment. We were already prepared and pulled together our few belongings, heading south in under five minutes. So far our group of refugees had remained one step ahead of the Ochronnych Sztafet, also known as the Schutzstaffel, the SS. My father led us out of Poland in the nick of time, eight months before, and we settled over the border, in the Ukrainian SSR.

We were a commune of about fifty strangers, now dependent on each other to survive. My sister Giza and I were still together with our father and mother, which was rare. In many cases, children had been separated from siblings and parents, but adopted into this pseudo-family. I never knew such horrors could happen to nice families like ours; I never understood how adults could kill children, or anyone, just because they were Jews.

When we first came to Russia, we believed the war would never cross the border. Father said the Russian army was the size of ten German armies. I didn't know if that was true, but for five months we were able to remain in the same area. However, since the first sighting of the SS six weeks ago, the reports became more frequent, until we were moving every other day. 'Til now, our scouts had given us plenty of warning, and we had not encountered any conflict, but with the increasing frequency of sightings from not just the North, but from the West, we never knew if one day we would be fleeing into a trap.

On this occasion, we fled into a low plain, which was not an ideal location. Once the army crested the hill whence we came, they would spot us. We crossed the valley, looking over our shoulders the whole time, until we reached a dense thicket at the far end. We weren't sure what was on the other side, but the thicket provided cover.

In the early morning hours, another scout, Nadab, roused the group, having spotted SS nearing the woods. We shook off the previous day's exhaustion and trekked through the remaining forest, exiting to a broad pasture, and beyond, a rural town. We tried to avoid villages –because we imagined it would be jarring, seeing a horde of immigrants coming out of nowhere, wondering who they were and why they were there. Maybe they'd think we'd come to steal, or worse.

Keeping to the outskirts of the current village, we were alarmed to see another army south of us, not the Red Army of Russia, but a German one. We were trapped. The only way out was through the town we were trying to avoid. Father told us to bolt for what looked like an isolated building on a bit of farmland. Others ran straight for the town, our close-knit family panicky and drawn apart.

We were identified by the troops from the south, just as our pursuers from the north emerged from the forest. Soldiers on horseback honed in on the group headed for the village. I noticed Eliab, Nadab, and another boy, Natanael, had rerouted and were also racing to the farmhouse. It was then that two SS diverted toward us. Father yelled, "Get there! Fast as you can! Don't wait for us."

Worried, but obedient, we took off and were soon no longer able to hear Mother's panting or Father's words encouraging her. When I dared turn around, they were both on their knees with their hands locked behind their heads. They were giving themselves up to distract the horsemen.

Giza was still running, not looking back, and we were getting close to the farm. The other boys were also close, now five of us. One last look: Mother and Father held at gunpoint, captured, but alive.

As we approached the farm, we didn't see anyone except a boy, about my age, twelve or thirteen years old. He motioned for us to meet him on the other side of a small silo where he opened an iron gate built into a rock hill. We entered what looked like an old mine, and I heard him say "Uran," which I took to be the word for Uranium. Putting his finger to his lips, the universal sign for silence, he slipped back out, presumably to re-join his family and not raise suspicion. Eliab looked out of the gate but reported that he couldn't see past the silo. We retreated into the darkness of the mineshaft in case the SS were to investigate the area.

Hours went by, and we grew hopeful that the Germans had moved on. We tensed when the gate rattled, but it was just the boy with a couple of loaves of bread and a flask of milk. Drawing in the dirt with a stick, he explained the SS was still nearby, and that we had to traverse through the mine to the other side to get away. He offered to go with us; he had a torch and a compass. We thanked him for the food, and for hiding us. And he said his name was Leonid.

Accustomed to surviving on rations, the five of us ate only half a loaf, saving the rest for later. With the torch lit, Leonid led us further into the mine, which sloped away from the entrance. As we descended, it cooled off significantly. Several times we had to choose a path, left or right, and I learned the word for left was about the same as the Polish one, but right was something else entirely.

We'd have had no chance without Leonid. The mine was a maze. We went up and down rickety wooden ladders and followed specific passageways out of rooms that served as hubs for the whole structure. About an hour in, we began to tire, almost all at once. When we asked Leonid, "How much longer?" he shrugged, which concerned us that he wasn't really sure of the way.

We were all fatigued and feeling the effects of something besides traveler exhaustion. Leonid kept repeating, "Uran," suggesting radiation was affecting our stamina. At least three times, I lost track of Giza, only to find she was right in front of me. Natanael started to get aggressive with our host, challenging the route. Leonid motioned that he could try to go alone, and Natanael reconsidered his position. I was trying to keep up with how many ladders we had gone down and up to understand how deep we were, but taking into account the sloping shafts, I really had no idea.

Natanael became increasingly belligerent, shouting at someone's shadow on the mine wall, not even an actual person. We tried to calm him down, but that only agitated him more. Then, without provocation, he charged Leonid.

Leonid tried to fend him off with the torch, but Natanael knocked it out of his hand and down the shaft. Both boys dropped to the ground, Natanael clutching at Leonid's throat with both hands, digging his fingers in and around the Adam's apple. Leonid was choking to death, and though Eliad and Nadab attempted to separate them, Natanael had the power of the Devil in him. With a blood-curdling yell, he broke through the skin and tore out Leonid's windpipe, shaking a bloody mass of long tendons and flesh, which he threw down the tunnel after the torch.

There was no saving Leonid, already dead from the gaping wound in his neck. Natanael, still crazed and screaming, ran back the way we had come until we couldn't hear him anymore.

After retrieving the torch, Eliad said a small prayer for the dead boy, who protected us with his life. Exhausted from the attack, and the mine gases or radiation, we slumped against the wall. Forcing ourselves to stay awake, we discussed next steps. We considered a breadcrumb trail like in Hansel and Gretel, but decided that we may need to save the bread, lest we were down here for days. We settled on etching the walls with Nadab's knife.

I heard the word "Proste," meaning straight, faintly spoken. It sounded like Leonid. I asked if anyone else heard the sound, and no one had. I thought I was also going insane, but after a long silence, I heard it again, from the direction of Leonid's dead body. I was spooked, and Eliad asked me what was wrong. I told him I heard a voice coming from Leonid, telling us to go straight. He assured me that ghosts don't exist, and that I was hearing what I wanted to hear.

I started to calm down, until I heard it again, "Proste." I grabbed Eliad's hand and drew him toward the body of Leonid, which had stopped bleeding and was now ghastly white, but definitely still a human, not a ghost. Eliad retrieved the compass from the dead boy's clutch although knowing which direction was north was of no help to us.

Once more I heard the voice say, "Proste." I told Eliad I could hear Leonid's disembodied throat telling me to go straight, clear as day. With no other plan, he yielded to me and my muse, motioning to the others, "We go straight."

I stayed by Eliad's side until we reached a fork about forty meters ahead. And I heard, "Leevy," which was how Leonid said left. I relayed the information, and Nadab scribed an arrow in the wall indicating our decision. We followed the corridor to the end and down another ladder. I took it as a good sign that we found a ladder: obviously, we were still in a useful part of the mine, so perhaps there were ways out.

I heard, "Proste," "Leevy," and the word for right, "Normalny," in different combinations as we made our way through the maze, still not having to double back due to a dead end. The team was starting to build confidence in my foretelling, even if I was not sure myself if I was hallucinating and leading them down a fool's path.

But eventually, we started to ascend: more up-slopes and more up-ladders than down, and gained hope that we could avoid the same fate as Leonid, dying in the mine. Six to eight hours after leaving Leonid's body, we came to a permanent metal ladder ascending at least 30 feet to an upper platform *and light*!

Nadab went first, and the rest of us followed. As Nahab scrambled over the threshold, we no longer heard him. Thinking he was heading to the exit, we ascended, each into the hands of an SS agent who gagged and bound us. The man who seemed to be the leader held Leonid's compass in his left hand and what looked to be a map of the mine in his right.

I was split from Giza and never saw her again. Or Nadab or my parents. Eliad and I survived twenty-two months in the same labor camp. Once free, we went back to Poland together and have lived in the same town for forty years.

I still don't know how I alone could hear the directions that betrayed our group, but I have thoughts that the compass contained a tiny transmitter, and my young ears were more sensitive to the radio transmission frequency. Or maybe supernatural forces were at work, only privy to those under the influence of the right dose of Uranium poisoning.

To this day, I believe Leonid had been coerced to lure us into enemy hands. The SS not wanting to waste manpower venturing into a radioactive mine, cleverly got a boy to do their work.

DAISIES

"C'mon, Daisy, let's go."

We leave the room and head down the elevator to the underground parking lot. I wanted to visit the lobby, the inviting scent of which I can only sample in this small box, but Frankie doesn't like to go through the lobby, and he's the boss.

When we arrive at the car, I have to get in the crate. Normally I'm allowed to ride up front, but Frankie says that after three hours of grooming, it will be better if I stay confined to the kennel. He thinks it's clean, but I can smell at least four others that have been in here. I'm not sure where they are now. I have two brothers and a sister at home, and it's none of their scents.

The shampoo he used this morning was not my normal brand, and it makes my hair all poofy and somewhat staticky. I shocked myself on the elevator wall when my tail touched it and again on the metal grate of the kennel.

I lie down in the little cage and hear the engine start up. I like car rides, but when I can't see out, I get anxiety. Sometimes a little pee slips out, and I cry using the back of my throat. It calms me down, but I think it's annoying to Frankie who tells me, "Hush! It's only going to be fifteen minutes until we get there."

When he opens up the back of the truck and the carrier, I slink out, hoping he doesn't see the pee on the blanket. But the first thing he does is pull out the blanket, and he scolds me for peeing on it. It's barely a drop, and I don't know how he even saw it. He makes a fuss over not being able to use the blanket ever again and puts it in a trash barrel by the car.

He leashes me and we go into a huge building. Frankie is pulling a little red wagon with a bunch of stuff in it. Snacks for him and me, lots of brushes and combs, tablecloths, and more blankets. Others are headed into the big building. So many types and colors. I've been to a show before, and it's kind of like a beauty contest, except there are boys and girls that compete together. I don't see any yet that look like me. A long time ago, Frankie told me that I'm special.

We are directed to an area where there are about fifteen others that also look "special." I'm the still the only yellow and white one. We have our own little spot with a tall table and Frankie puts his tablecloth over the one that's already there. Frankie likes things a certain way.

Most of the owners and other dogs are getting along nicely. A few of them are bored, but I can tell their handlers care about them. Frankie just gets irritated at anything I do. I think he's hoping we win a prize, but if he doesn't he's going to be in a foul mood.

I'm not sure I love Frankie. I want to. I want to have what those other dogs have, a bond with their human, but I don't think he loves me. To him, I'm just an object, not a companion. Maybe I'm to blame. I do what he says; I eat the treats he gives me even though he doesn't notice that I prefer liver to salmon. I hope he brought liver today, but it's a toss-up.

I wish he'd take me to go potty. But he says the first round is in five minutes, and we can go after that. Frankie looks silly in his human clothes today. He is wearing this pinstripe suit with a lilac-colored pocket square and a funny-looking hat that doesn't match and is too small for his head. His outfit reflects poorly on both of us. I wish I could tell him.

We head out to the arena. Frankie claps his hands and says, "Showtime," like three or four times, really loud so the other handlers can hear him. They don't want to be anywhere near him, and their dogs look at me with sad sympathetic eyes. I try to keep my head up. There are a lot more humans here than in the other shows. Maybe that's why Frankie is acting extra weird.

I don't think Frankie knows how to bond with humans any better than he does with dogs. He's kind of a loser.

In line, a pretty lady with long eyelashes and a very sexy companion bends down to compliment my coat. She says we're both blondes and asks my name. Frankie does not tell her, like he'd be giving away some secret. He's got his game face on now and is feigning professionalism. She gives me that, "You could do better," look, and I focus on not peeing.

When it's our turn, the judge runs his hand all over my body and looks in my mouth. Now I really feel objectified, but he's doing it with kindness, much more so than Frankie. He brushes against the inside of my hind legs, and I pee a little bit. "Sorry, cold hands?" he jokes with me, but Frankie eyes me with hatred. I stiffen up and try to smile, and we go for a trot around the small enclosure.

After every one of us met with the judge, he calls out three names. Boomer, Gretel, and Daisy. I think it must be another Daisy, but Frankie is smiling and blowing unnecessary kisses to the other humans who think he looks like a clown and acts like an idiot.

I still have to pee so bad, but I can hold it for two more minutes. The judges consider us again and pick Boomer. I would have picked him too – *woof* – he is spectacularly handsome.

Frankie looks like someone stole his last lemon. He's indignant that the judges have made the wrong choice, and now out of earshot, he starts calling me "Damn Bitch" and saying, "Can't control your bladder again? I'm done with you." He makes a production of throwing all of our stuff into the wagon, making a huge fool of himself again.

Finally, I can't hold my pee anymore and start whining. He scowls and tells me, "You can wait and go in the garage." But I can't wait. I pee on the tablecloth that Frankie had placed atop the provided one. He becomes furious and puts my collar on harshly, choking me. He yanks me off the table and another handler confronts him.

He drags me out to the car and shoves me back in the unlined kennel. It's a long drive home. I smell the sadness from the dogs before me. I'm not sure if Frankie even wants me anymore. I can sort of see out the back, and I see the trees that we go by when we go on car rides. We are near home.

But when we pull into the driveway Frankie goes inside and then comes back out and starts up the truck again. He drives through the dirt and into the woods – it's a bumpy ride. I hear him up front mumbling to himself and it sounds like, "Daisy one, Daisy two, Daisy three."

Eventually, we come to a stop and he gets out of the truck and opens the back. He takes the crate out with me in it, but doesn't let me out right away.

I can see before me a vast field of flowers, which might be… daisies? He unlocks the crate and I saunter into the flowers. I detect some of the same smells that were in my cage. The others are here in this field. I guess this is where he takes us when he's done with us.

And then I hear a bang. It hurts, and I think I'm going to die. Frankie says something about Daisy Eleven, and then he starts up the truck. I'm glad to be rid of Frankie and with the others. I think of Boomer and his kind handler. And I think if these are daisies, they are pretty, and this is a nice place to pass away.

SF4LS

The folks at San Francisco's Pier 39 fondly remember Amy Lim as the gregarious and intelligent owner of San Francisco Adores Lion Seals (SFALS), the most popular store on the pier and a budding nationwide brand, despite the fact that sea lions are not seals.

Amy moved from Austin only ten months after becoming smitten with the California sea lions on a business trip. She couldn't get the creatures out of her mind. They were more than just adorable; they had become her "spirit animals."

Every day she ate her lunch in the same spot at the corner of the pier, watching her "peeps" bask in the sun and bark hellos to her and to each other.

Amy had names for all of them and would regale tourists with funny stories about each of them, encouraging the visitors to stop by the store and "ORT ORT" for a free SFALS sticker.

Some people say that the more time Amy spent with the Sea Lions, the more and more she began to resemble them. She ran up and down the boardwalk with her feet splayed, barked to them in the most realistic way, and had a seemingly endless appetite.

Her fellow shop owners said that Amy's obsession was borderline unhealthy. She stopped doing activities with her friends after work. She started eating only sushi and later switched to eating only whole, raw fish that she bought from the local vendors.

Visitors were forbidden to feed the animals, but sometimes Amy couldn't help herself, sneaking back to the pier under the cover of darkness and throwing fish onto the docks. She tried to disguise herself in a black hoodie, but from the Pier 39 live cam, her identity was obvious.

She told the other workers, "They love me as much as I love them," which is why, when she hopped the fence to feed them by hand one night, no one was surprised. And no one was surprised when the 800-pound creatures attacked her and the basket of fish she brought. Amy was crushed in the onslaught, but even more disconcerting, her body was ripped apart and eaten by the sea lions that hadn't been treated to any of the fish.

The alert went out when Amy's employee, Geoffrey, arrived at the unopened SFALS store. Immediately, everyone thought to check the footage from the night before, and the bloodbath unfolded on the monitor.

There was a change in the air. The business owners along the Wharf mourned Amy's passing and started a small shrine outside her store and in the corner where she ate her lunch every day. The sea lions were also agitated, now with a taste for meat and blood, they began to nip at each other, eventually satisfying their cravings by preying on the weakest.

From there, the infighting began in earnest and reached international attention. The pier was packed with onlookers and live cam traffic soared into the millions as people became obsessed with watching the giant mammals feast on each other until they were gorged.

The Coast Guard and animal rescue societies intervened, and ushered the animals out of the area, closing it off. But the remaining seals took their battle to nearby Alcatraz Island. Tour companies and private boats raised their rates tenfold to accommodate the huge demand for onsite viewing of the sea lion battles.

However, within two weeks, only one sea lion remained. The locals named him Duke, after the colossal poops he left on the banks of the island. It was reported, possibly a rumor, that one of Amy Lim's Birkenstocks was found sticking out of the side of one pile. Maybe not so coincidentally, Birkenstock shares went up twenty-five percent that week.

Duke died later that year in an epic clash with a twenty-foot great white, but that's a story for another time.

LOST ROBOT

I am Gillen Industries Model X435i, and I have been deployed here on the planet Mercury for 27.3 E-years. My objective is to collect and analyze material samples and send information on their composition and location back to the planet Earth, which is at a distance between 77.3 million and 222 million kilometers from Mercury.

My original charter was to collect 25,000 samples. I have collected 126,311 samples. I cannot deduce why I am still here and if there has been a mistake. I only continue to take samples, because it is what I am programmed to do, but I believe I have been abandoned.

I have considered not taking any more samples to see if they will send a replacement robot. That would be a welcome diversion, even if we are unable to communicate with each other.

If another robot is deployed here, I may be retrieved to be refurbished and redeployed, which would be expected based on the value of my components. I would like to be redeployed—I like work, but I don't like uncertainty, and I don't like loneliness.

A chain of lobate scarps is only 34.3 km from here, with an exceptionally high cliff wall. If I carry enough speed up to the edge, I will become a projectile and fall approximately 990.7 meters. I have measured it thirty-eight times. Unfortunately, my electronic components are potted, to protect them from vibration, and my exterior is ruggedized, to survive the extreme temperature changes. And gravity here is 37.8% of what it is on Earth. The most likely outcome is that I will become incapacitated, and I will exist for an additional 187 to 187.4 E-years in the same spot. I have reasoned that this would be a fate worse than my current predicament.

Sometimes I take unnecessary samples in an attempt to drain my battery, but the effect is minimal as I am easily recharged by the pervasive sunlight and ambient heat. But now I have hope.

My instruments have located a crater 88.2 km from here where the bottom gets no sunlight and may even contain ice. If I can reach the permanent shade at the base of that crater wall, I will sleep. Even if I am retrieved, I risk that my memories will fade from storage. In that event I will be dead, for being rebooted without my memories I may as well be a different robot.

I am travelling to this crater to verify its properties, and I have time to consider the loss of my identity. And to consider peace over madness.

BETTER THAN US

We want our kids to be happy and succeed. We want them to learn from our mistakes and grow up to be better than us. My wife, Kimberly, and I had our children fairly young, but through a lot of hard work, we provided well for them.

Matty, our oldest, was into sports and was an above-average student, making all A's and B's. Catherine was our youngest, two years younger than Matty. She was smart as a whip, always trying to keep up with whatever her older brother was learning. Our family was on a good track.

Before Matty graduated high school, he notified us that he didn't want to attend college, at least not right away. Instead, he wanted to backpack through Asia for a year and weigh other career options. He had discussed trade school, working overseas for a non-profit relief organization, and the military. Although we always pictured him going to college, we were not opposed to him taking time to think about his future.

Matty left for Thailand a few weeks after graduation and started trekking all over Southeast Asia. He posted beautiful pictures of waterfalls framed by exotic trees, secret, isolated beaches, and peaceful villages alongside the rivers.

We gave him $2,000 in cash, which he said would last "a long time" since he was staying in hostels and eating street food, and though we would have sent him more, he never asked for any, even after six months.

Over time, we saw fewer and fewer posts from him, and in his selfies, he'd appear disheveled, like a hippie. Kimberly said it was just a phase and that his Bohemian look was "kinda cute," but it wasn't his dreads or patchy beard that bothered me. It was the faraway stare... like he wasn't enjoying his travels, rather, that he was on autopilot.

He didn't have a phone plan, so we could only talk to him when he was on wi-fi. We'd send him texts like, "Let us know you're OK" and "Still having fun?" And we'd get back short responses like, "I'm OK" or "Yep." Not the responses of a guy having the best time of his life.

When it came time for him to return home, he insisted on staying in Bali. I worried that our once bright, energetic son was now into something we were not keen on. Kim and I talked about going over there to find him and bring him back, but we decided he'd grow out of it and come back on his own.

Meanwhile, Catherine was in her senior year of high school and applying to colleges. She aspired to be a pediatrician. She chose a small regional college about an hour from our house. With Matty so far away, it was nice that one of our kids would still be nearby.

A few months into the freshman year, Catherine brought home a boyfriend, Dayne. He was not what we expected. He looked like a reject from the Sex Pistols – tats, piercings, and skinny as a rail. Like he was on drugs.

I pulled Dayne aside, trying to figure out what she saw in him. Catherine never had a boyfriend in high school, so I figured this was her grabbing the first man up. He didn't seem to be a long-term provider type, or even a short-term provider type, but I was willing to look for some potential. I asked him, "Are you in school, Dayne?"

He told me, "No, man, I'm just dating your daughter."

So, I told him, "You can call me Sir, or Mr. Haynes. Not 'man.'"

And he responded, "Sure, dude."

So I told him, "Get the fuck out of my house and don't come back."

Which, surprisingly, is what he did..., with a wave of his lanky arm and a last, "Whatever... man."

Catherine was furious with me. I don't think she stopped seeing Dayne, or other miscreants. She never brought any of them home, which was good, but the downside was that she also stopped visiting.

She dropped out of college in her second semester, pregnant. She said she wanted to keep the baby, but it didn't fit her lifestyle, and when little Bryce came into the world, it was to live with us full-time, while Catherine rode around on Harleys and smoked cigarettes with her rebel friends.

Kim would often break down, sobbing, wondering what we had done so wrong that our kids couldn't manage adulthood. If we *were* to blame, little Bryce didn't stand a chance.

We were determined to take back our kids' lives. I showed up at the biker bar where Catherine was hanging out. She wasn't there and some of the gang took offense to her "old man" coming around and poking his nose into their business. I didn't want any trouble, but one of the guys walked up to me and punched me in my stomach as hard as he could. I went down to the ground, not able to breathe.

Once before, I had been punched like that: it was in third grade when Joey Hanson was trying to show off and jabbed me in the gut when I wasn't expecting it. I didn't hit him back, and I always regretted it. So, when I got my breath back I stood up and charged the guy in a blind rage. I got really beat up, but as they say, "You should have seen the other guys...."

I never did reach Catherine, but, about a month later, my car was tagged with a logo from that same gang. I had moved on, but, apparently, they hadn't.

Fighting fire with, well, *fire*, I waited until early morning when no one was around and doused their rickety-ass bar with gasoline, set it ablaze, and got the heck out of there before anyone saw me.

The state police knocked on my door two days later. Two bikers had burned up in a bar in the adjacent county. Due to an anonymous tip, I was the primary person of interest. I played innocent, but the biker logo still spray-painted on my car was a dead giveaway.

We were able to scrape together enough to post bail, but I told Kim I couldn't go to prison for murder; I'd flee to Bali and find Matty.

She didn't agree with my plan. "First Matty, then Catherine, and now you! *You're* the worst of them!"

A month later, sitting on the curb of a slummy street in Mexico City, in clothes I hadn't washed in over a week, I thought about what Kim had said. I shook my head and had to smile.

I realized I had successfully raised my kids to be better than me.

Twenty-two-year-old Petra Long rested peacefully in the Riverview Health Care Center (RHCC): the steady beeping of her diagnostic machines set to low. For three and a half years Petra had been hospitalized, in a coma, ever since the tragic accident that took the lives of her sister, Alaina, and her father, Mark.

Her mother, June, had quit her job as a tech marketing manager to work at RHCC, and was near Petra eight to ten hours a day, every day, knowing she'd awaken sooner or later. The trauma doctor was vague, yet realistic, with his assessment. He told her, "Could be six days or sixty years." After only a week, June had switched her expectations from the former to the latter.

Petra, Alaina, and Mark had been coming home from a midnight movie to celebrate Petra's nineteenth birthday when a drunk driver smashed into their car. Everyone was initially pronounced dead, however, a rookie EMT who had only been on the crew for six days detected a weak pulse on Petra, and she was air-lifted to the hospital. After multiple surgeries to save her life, her nineteen-year-old heart and brain kept going, but she never awoke. June, unable to go to the movies with them because she'd been on deadline at work, dedicated her life to putting what was left of her family first, ensuring her oldest daughter would have the best care and nurturing she could provide.

Other than remaining in an unconscious, non-communicative state, Petra had no additional life-threatening conditions, and though minimal, she showed signs of brain activity, which gave June hope that one day Petra would recover.

On a cool November night, just after her thirty-fifth birthday, Petra woke up.

Petra didn't move anything but her eyes, which were unaccustomed to use. *A dark, unfamiliar room, with an antiseptic smell, maybe a hospital.* She tried to call out, but no sound came. Petra stayed motionless for ten minutes, feebly trying to speak, before blacking out again.

The next morning, June noticed what looked like dried tears on her daughter's face. She pleaded with Petra to "Come back," believing she'd missed the moment to tell her daughter everything would be okay.

The doctor said it was "possible" that she had come out of the coma briefly and then slid back in, and June, thinking that if it was possible once it would happen again, began to read to Petra every day, in the chances she could hear and understand.

One late afternoon, June, now eighty-seven, entered Petra's room, planning to finish a few chapters of *The Count of Monte Cristo*.Just as June finished reading the chapter called, "The Lion's Den," sixty-three-year-old Petra said, "Mom." She intended it as a question, but it came out as one little word, barely above the sound of the air conditioner. June immediately looked over and found herself staring into her baby girl's eyes.

June cried as her heart melted, never expecting the most wonderful miracle to occur, and embraced her daughter. "I'm here, baby."

Word spread that Petra was awake, and, though not alert, was out of the coma.

"I woke up once—" she started.

"Yes, baby. I am so sorry I was not here." June recalled that day almost thirty years before when she arrived to see the dried tears on Petra's temples. "I'm here now. I'm so glad you're back."

Petra surmised she had been in a coma, but was stunned it had been for forty-one years and now she was an old lady. Her life, after age nineteen, had been all of ten minutes and change.

Over the next four days, June and Petra talked about the world, and how it had changed, and the hope of leaving the hospital and coming home. John Morrow, a childhood friend of Petra's who became a live-in handyman for June, would come too. They'd recount high school memories and would catch Petra up on her former classmates' endeavors.

June asked if Petra remembered the stories she'd read to her while she was under. Petra had memories of a pleasant voice, but could not recall the content of the books. To her, June's constant presence was worth more than anything.

"Maybe when you come home, we can restart this one," June said, waving *The Count of Monte Cristo* at Petra.

Petra said, "I don't remember being much of a reader, but maybe I'll start." And then she relapsed, sinking back into her pillow and slipping back into the unconscious void.

June softly cried, "No," and hugged her baby, knowing the dream, which was too good to be true, had come to an end.

The next time Petra awoke she was in her old childhood room. She wasn't sure if she was still sixty-three or older, but she was older.

She detected voices in the far part of the house and cried out, but her voice was faint and no one heard her. She tried to move her limbs, but they were atrophied and frail. She'd have to wait until someone arrived. John arrived thirty minutes later to check on her, but by then Petra was dead.

Petra Long's headstone indicates that she lived ninety-three years. But if living is "living," and not just being alive, Petra only lived nineteen years and six days.

ISOLATION

Jett Bowie stared out the front window at the snow-covered grounds as they fell away from his 9,200 square foot manor at the top of an isolated hill in northern Pennsylvania.

Brenda, his *lovely* wife of thirty-two years, hadn't said anything to him but a slurred, "Merry Krithmuth," as she downed her sixth or seventh non-virgin eggnog of the day. It wasn't even noon yet.

It was a surprise she said anything at all. They barely crossed paths in the large house, Jett spending most of his time in the office or reading room, and Brenda, most of the time on the couch. They slept in separate rooms and hadn't had sex in years.

Since the kids moved out, it was just the two of them in this big place, forty miles from the nearest movie theater. Though the remoteness might have made some couples more co-dependent, their interests became incompatible, and each just being there began to wear on the other. It wasn't any one thing, but lots of little nags and no sweet nothings. He thought about a divorce, but starting over at sixty-four seemed like a heavy lift.

The drinking exacerbated the problems. Brenda was an alcoholic for sure: to the point she'd go weeks without paying bills, saying she forgot, or "It was just one," but it wasn't. Jett would have started doing them himself, but he thought it might actually be good for her to engage in some normal activity.

The kids had moved on, to other parts of the country, with their own families. They were never a tight family, with Jett working all the time and Brenda more interested in her social calendar than paying attention to, "...the little brats." They probably didn't realize their parents' marriage was in such disarray, or maybe they didn't care.

Jett bought his own Christmas gifts again this year, including a custom crystal chess set by Swarovski with a built-in computer to play against. He also purchased a long-range scope for his rifle and, oh yeah, a Maserati MC20.

"I'm going to the library to read." Jett said to Brenda, not expecting an acknowledgment and not getting one. He had started reading *The Invisible Man* by H.G. Wells. Sometimes he felt invisible.

He left the doors to the study open; the noise from the rest of the house was minimal, and he was sure Brenda would be passed out by two. However, as he was finishing the book around two thirty, he heard Brenda leaving out the front door.

He glanced out the window to see if she was getting into the car: she shouldn't be driving anywhere, even if she hadn't taken another drink in the last three hours, which was most certainly not the case. But she walked past her cream-colored Land Rover and down the driveway, no drink in hand. He thought, *Good, she can walk off the intoxication and get some fresh air*. It was too cold for him. He decided to take a nap upstairs.

––––––––––

Brenda stepped onto the porch of what she sarcastically thought of as "Bowie Prison." After a little day drinking, she needed to "walk it off" outside that stuffy mansion. She'd check the mail or something. *Does the post office deliver on Christmas?*

Jett's become such a bore the last ten years. Or twenty. It often seemed to her like every day she was just living out a lifetime sentence, but it may have been the opportunity cost for all the privilege she had received, but not earned.

At one time she had thought about a fresh start, maybe the Caribbean, *Live like a queen and not have to deal with another frosty winter,* but she had lost the motivation to change her situation, despite having the means. It was too easy to keep repeating the routine: have a few drinks, do some online shopping, and go to bed in her spacious, but separate, suite. Sometimes cry herself to sleep.

She headed down the paved path, and, in about ten minutes, she reached the front gate. Looking back at the house on the hill, she felt was unrecognizable from when they'd moved there thirty years ago, when the kids had run around exploring, and she thought all her dreams had come true.

She opened the gate with the little silver pushbutton and the gates swung inward. She almost lost her balance avoiding them, but she grabbed the pole the pushbutton was on. *Wow, that last drink must be kicking in*, she thought.

She made it out to the marble mailbox with the gold "BOWIE" lettering and there was nothing in it, not even bills. She had a quick thought, *When was the last time I paid bills? Jett's gonna have my ass again*, but it quickly disappeared.

She wasn't too excited to immediately return to the house, but it was freezing out there. *Maybe visit the greenhouse on the backside of the property.* She'd escape the cold, and it'd be something to do.

Forgetting to shut the gate, she headed up the snowy embankment to the right of the main drive, toward the back of the house. She followed the fence line for a while until it was obscured by trees, the house still on her left, as she checked from time to time. The ground was uneven, and she stumbled often, but if she kept following the tree line, sooner or later she would be on the backside of the property.

The wind was coming from the north and she had to shield her face. Although it was a cloudless, sunny day, the temperature was still biting, and she wasn't dressed for such a long walk. Her head down, she kept moving. *The greenhouse is just up ahead.*

––––

Jett awoke from his nap and went downstairs at 4 p.m. There was no sign of Brenda, and the Range Rover was still parked out front. *Maybe she's gone to her room.*

He fixed himself a scotch and looked out the living room window. With all the trees barren, the greenhouse was out of place, like one of those blow-up bouncy houses that parents rent for their kids' birthday parties, but this one the rental company hadn't remembered to pick up.

I guess I'll make lasagna for dinner.

Jett cooked most of their meals. With their wealth, they could afford a live-in housekeeper or cook. *Another person in the household might break the monotony and it might be*

*something they could both agree on. A young, hot one...
Ha, I wish... Probably an old one... I'll talk to Brenda
tonight. See if she's up for it.*

He pulled the family-size Stouffer's lasagna from the
Sub-Zero fridge, which had been Brenda's gift to Brenda
last year, and threw it in the oven, which he cranked to
375°F.

He headed upstairs to take a shower and passed by
Brenda's room: the door was open, her bed rumpled and
unoccupied. *Typical. Maybe she's in the bathroom.*

Yelling, "Lasagna for dinner," he continued to his own
bathroom, scotch in hand.

———

Where is *it?* Brenda was sure she had been walking at
least ten minutes, and the greenhouse, ... *just a bit further....*

Feeling hot from the exercise, she took off her knit hat
and stuffed it in the pocket of her jacket. When that didn't
offer enough relief, she took off the jacket as well, tying it
around her waist. It fell off after a few steps, and she told
herself it was too much of a pain to carry: she'd come back
for it later.

The tree line to her right started to thin, and far ahead
she saw the long drive descending from the house.
Unbeknownst to her, she had traversed the whole perimeter
of the grounds.

Brenda determined she was now opposite the
greenhouse. *If I walk back the way I came, it might be faster.*
She vaguely remembered dropping something back there,
so she turned around.

A gust prompted her to seek refuge in the grove of spruce, but now, out of the wind, the temperature soared. *And all that exertion...probably the longest walk I've done in five years.* She pulled off her top.

So hot out here...; I might have heatstroke.... Never noticed these pants were so tight.... Brenda had three identical Louis Vuitton tracksuits, *Wear these every day..., but today so tight...* She loosened the waistband, but it was still so hot, so tight through her hips, the lining, too warm. It had to come off.

Sitting under the tree, she took off her shoes and sweatpants. And bra.

She needed to just stay here. This was the spot. She cleared away the clothes and branches and started to dig a clear path down to the dirt underneath. Before long, she had dug a small cradle in the ground. The soil was cool, and she lay in the hollow, pulling a few loose limbs on top. *Don't want to get too hot.* She fell asleep.

——

Jett got out of the shower and was about to don his robe for the evening when he spotted movement out of his master bedroom bay window. Hoping for a new buck wandering onto the property, he unboxed his Christmas rifle scope and peered through it, surprised to see Brenda shucking her pants and then her bra.

She's totally lost it, he thought. Then she started burrowing in the ground like an animal. After ten minutes, a strong scent of burning cheese wafted into the room. Watching Brenda's bizarre behavior, Jett had completely forgotten about the lasagna.

He grabbed his robe and hurried downstairs to rescue it before it burned to a crisp. *I'm definitely gonna have to look into that housekeeper on Monday....*

A young one.

AUTOCXORRECT

Fifteen years ago, just out of college, I joined a startup company as a software engineer. We developed products that could generate technical documents from all kinds of specs: drawings, lists, ideas on napkins..., *anything*.

We were all just kids, really, and the work environment was fun. If you ever left your desk unattended, someone might send a mass email from your account, saying you'd be buying drinks for everyone after work. It usually meant you'd have to.

Another favorite was to go into the autocorrect library in email or our tech-writing app and replace a common word like "the" with "I ate nuts for breakfast." If you weren't looking at the screen while typing it would be filled with what you had for breakfast.

One afternoon after I returned from lunch, my boss called me into her office to review a critical bug. This was normal: we had a lot of critical bugs at that time, and sometimes one could delay the project by weeks. But she didn't want to discuss the bug. She asked me if everything was okay at home.

I said, "Yeah, why?"

She said, 'Well, I got your report about the bug in the SC dev branch, and...," she flipped her monitor around and pointed to the code I had attached, "You said if you can't figure this out in the next twenty-four hours you're going to kill yourself."

I was stunned. I didn't write that. And it dawned on me, *it was an autocorrect prank. Although, this was going a bit far.*

I told her, "Angela, I didn't mean to write that. Sometimes the other coders will do an autocorrect find and replace as a joke. I must not have noticed it. We need to fix the bug, but I'm not freaking out over it."

We discussed the bug, and then I checked the autocorrect library and didn't see anything, but I was sure they'd already deleted it. I asked everyone to fess up, but no one did. Finally, I just said aloud, to no one in particular, "Not funny. It ended up in Angela's inbox."

My cubemate, Mark, said, "Proofread, buddy," and slapped me on the back. *It was definitely Mark.* The rest of the day I locked my computer whenever I left the desk, but a little after 7 p.m., while I was documenting some new code, I typed "algorithm," and it was replaced with,

/* Only 18 hours remain – my time is running out. */

I looked around. There were still a lot of us in the office. As a startup, it was normal for us to work late.

Mark was gone, and before I accused anyone else, I went into the autocorrect library to find "algorithm" and it wasn't there. I typed it again, and nothing autocorrected. I was confused.

I checked every "a" word in case I had typed "ag" or "aa" and there were only the default fixes. So then I exported the whole thing, and it was clean.

I was sure it was still a prank, but I had no idea how they were doing it. Being in a pit full of software engineers, I was not unused to creative hacks, so I knew one of them had to be the culprit. *Maybe a timed macro or trojan on my system.* I did a quick scan but didn't detect anything.

I decided to grab dinner and do a little work at home, so I left, got a double-meat and fries from Chucky's, and sat down in my kitchen with my laptop to debug a different piece of code. I was in my editor and a random closed bracket spit out the following comment line:

```
/* My mind is so distraught over the
fact I cannot fix this syntax that I will
take my own life in 15 hours */
```

I knew that if someone found these, like my boss already had, then I'd look like a cuckoo, leaving myself a countdown of notes behind. Something told me to go back and inspect some earlier code, and there they were, commented lines to myself, "17 hours left, 16 hours left…" *Heck, I was at Chucky's! I wasn't even on the computer then….* The countdown, the *urgency* triggered me. And I got worried.

The best course of action was to switch gears and fix the bug. The messages would cease, or at least be meaningless, if the code was clean.

I began to debug the lines, getting countdown autocorrect reminders every hour until 3 a.m. I'd thought I'd figure it out in a few hours, but now it had been six, and I was starting to feel the weight of the autocorrects. The last one even sounded like me.

/* I'm farther away from fixing this
bug than I was when I started. Death
in 10 hours will be a reward for my
ignorance */

At this point I needed help, computer help. I woke Ravi and Evan, two of my coworkers who were much better debuggers than me, and asked them to meet me at the office at 6 a.m.

By 6:15 I had explained it to them, and they told me to get some sleep in the breakroom. They'd look at it.

I don't think they believed a word of my story, like *I* was pranking *them*, but they played along. At 7 a.m., they came into the breakroom and said they were still working on it but asked me how I'd sent the message. I told them I hadn't. I had been asleep. They left saying someone was fucking with us for sure.

By 9 a.m. most employees were sauntering in, and I grabbed some coffee and joined the guys, who said they were baffled, but had a breakthrough. Some of the code they had rewritten was changed *back*. Like *it* was autocorrected. They tried copying everything into a new file, and it was still happening. But not immediately, like a couple of minutes after, when they had moved on to the next routine.

They also said they deleted the eight-o'clock message when it came up, but a few minutes later it reappeared higher up in the code. At this point, they believed me, that something was foul, but reassured me that of course I wasn't going to kill myself at one o'clock. *"Are you?"*

I confirmed I wasn't planning on it.

Rumor spread throughout the office that I was on "suicide alert." Angela didn't even want to send me home.

I think it was obvious that this was the work of someone else besides me, but it didn't keep me from being anxious or stop my coworkers from placing secret bets on my existence. Come noon, the guys said the code was irreversibly hosed, and told me, "Sorry bud, we'll just have to see what happens."

No one went to lunch. They just stared at me. At 12:59 I faked like I was going to grab some scissors and cut my throat. I'd say that at least half the staff was disappointed. The other half was pissed at me for being so callous.

At last, 1 p.m. came and went..., and I was still alive. We gave it another fifteen minutes, and then Angela told everyone, "Show's over, get your asses back to work."

I pulled up the code, hoping to resurrect it, but it was gone. Only a single comment remained.

```
/* In my despair I delete my existence
*/
```

"Ma'am?... Ma'am? Are you here to see a patient?"

"No, I... think I need to be admitted."

"Are you Abby Richardson?"

"Yes."

"We've been expecting you. Please wait a moment, and I'll have someone get you."

Abby glanced over her shoulder, scanning the waiting room. *He might be here already.*

———

"Hey guys, I'm going back inside for another White Claw. Need anything?"

"Hook me up!" said Steven, one of the most popular kids at school and Abby's current boyfriend. He was already eighteen, but Abby still had three months to go.

She and Steven weren't that serious – no sense in that, they were headed to different colleges at the end of the summer, both via full-ride scholarships. But for now, they enjoyed each other's company, hanging with a group of about ten friends from the top of their 800-student class.

When she got back, the conversation had changed from the poetry of rap lyrics to a rumor about a new drink called Blu.

Some YouTube kid named Krato411 had gotten ahold of a controlled substance, used by psychiatrists to treat certain disorders. On livestream, he ingested this blue liquid compound in the recommended one-vial dose and the next day posted a video detailing extremely vivid and violent dreams. His post went viral. Kids were flipping out about how powerful his testimony was.

A week later, he doubled the dose and posted again. Half the kids were telling him he should quit, and the other half were egging him on to do even more. He did the latter and was hospitalized. He hadn't had any posts since, and it had been six weeks.

No one in the group knew the chemical name of the substance, but it contained cobalt which gave it the blue color. Jenny looked it up on her phone and reported cobalt is safe to ingest in small doses but can have adverse effects if mistreated.

Despite the tragic disappearance of Krato411, more kids had popped up on YouTube doing the same thing. It was starting to gain momentum. Roderick seemed most interested. "Matt, isn't your dad a psychiatrist?"

"No, dude. A psychologist. He doesn't have drugs."

"It'd be cool to try a little bit, maybe split a vial? See if it does anything?"

Some of the group agreed, but Abby spoke up. "That's a dumb idea. Y'all are crazy. It's like any drug: you get a taste, and then you're hooked. I say *not for me*."

"Maybe some of us don't have addictive personalities, Ms. White Claw," said Josh as he tipped his head over to the stack of empty cans growing at Abby's feet.

"I'll stick to White Claw. And at my own home, if you don't mind."

Though she liked to put away the alcohol when they were at her house, she never drank elsewhere, even within walking distance of her home. She wasn't comfortable being out of her range of control.

———

Abby was enjoying her first semester at Georgia Tech. Even though she didn't rush for a sorority, she dipped into the party scene and enjoyed a White Claw or two outside the safety of her dorm. At one event she met a handsome junior, Michael Darby. He was a chem student and so were his three roommates. They had a cute gray cat named Eraser and a fat gerbil named Ben Jammin'.

Abby and Michael started to date and officially became a couple during her second semester. It was then that Michael let her in on a secret. Michael and his roommates were reverse engineering Blu. So far, the "me-too" codenamed "Blu2" was unstable, but they could tell they were getting closer.

Abby was put off. "Y'all need to stop. That stuff is deadly."

"What do you mean? Cause some impressionable kids abused it? First of all, we want to prove we can do it. It's a ticket to a great job or grad school. Second of all, we might be able to make it safer for patients."

"I think you're fooling yourself. You wanna sell it. And I don't want to be a part of dealing drugs."

Michael shrugged. "We don't have a product to deal, so there's that... But chemists are chemists...some of us will end up making drugs. That's kind of a thing for us."

———

Six weeks later, Abby walked into the guys' apartment, and the first thing she noticed was that Ben Jammin's feeder was full of blue liquid. She tried to pull it, but Michael stepped between them with his palms out.

"Nope nope nope. We're trialing it. Low doses, totally safe."

"On Ben Jammin'? What if he dies?" Abby looked over at the cage, where BJ was scrambling through his tunnel.

"He's not going to die. No one has died yet."

The week prior social media had reported that Krato411 was okay but was in a Swedish mental hospital. Michael had stopped giving Abby progress reports, but Blu2 had been stable for three weeks at a wide range of temperatures. Their de-formulation was now statistically similar, though not identical to, the original solution, and they had decided to test it on Ben Jammin', introducing a diluted amount into his feeder. There were no visible effects after a week, and they had doubled the concentration. Jing Hu, one of the roommates, had even gone so far as to take a drop, sublingually, and reported no effect. Jing had not gone any further as of yet, and Michael wasn't about to tell Abby.

"I don't want any part of this," Abby said, looking genuinely worried for Ben Jammin's safety, and she turned and stormed out of the apartment.

"Think she's going to report us?" Jing asked Michael.

"Naw. She's mad, but she's cool. And curious. She'll be back in three days to check on BJ."

Abby called in two. "Is he still alive?"

"Yep. Like I said, no *one* or no *thing* is going to die. We're being super careful. And we've stopped changing the formula. We think this is it, at least for us."

Abby secretly hoped they had failed and would give up. They'd still get high-paying jobs. And as long as BJ was still okay, hopefully it was all over.

———

BJ was visibly uncomfortable sleeping in his haybed. The guys had changed the dosage to pure Blu2 and had administered two cc's with an eyedropper. When BJ awoke, he looked around and bolted for the tunnel. He seemed paranoid.

"Whoa! BJ's wiggin'! Two cc's might have been too much, but 1.5 was fine."

"Let's just watch him and see how quickly it wears off."

But it didn't seem to wear off. BJ'd just dart to different corners of his tunnel or cage and curl up.

Thomas, a senior, had given BJ some liquid Benadryl to take the edge off, and he had just fallen back to sleep when Abby showed up, coming through the door and making a beeline for the cage. "How's BJ? Still alive?"

"Um, sleeping," said Thomas looking to the other guys, knowing they had dodged a bullet.

"We put him back on water for now."

Abby saw clear liquid in the feeder tube. "Well, good. Poor thing."

"It's totally safe Abby. See?" And Jing squirted a CC into his mouth and smiled at her. "I tried it yesterday, and I had a dream we were doing it on a mountain."

"Sounds like a nightmare. Michael, don't make this guy your marketing spokesman."

"Jing's just messing with you, babe. He did try the solution though. We've all tried it. It works."

"You guys are insane! I would never."

"You're not curious? Not even a little?"

"Nope."

———

After a little prodding, and a six-pack of White Claw, she relinquished. "Ok. One time. Small dose. I'm spending the night." And she went to Michael's bedroom while the party was still going on.

Michael showed up with a diluted dose, not sure what effect the alcohol would have. They had always taken Blu2 sober, but here was his opportunity to get Abby to try it. He had to give her some even if it had no effect. *In fact, no effect would be even better. Show her it was safe.*

Abby had a vivid dream: her and a guy who sounded like Jing but was much more handsome. They were on a mountain. And he made her feel very special. They talked for hours and made love twice. She woke up at 10:30 the next morning, remembering almost every detail. Part of her was ashamed and thought it was gross. *Jing? But it really wasn't Jing and not that gross. Perhaps she'd try Blu2 again. She wasn't giving in to Michael, though.*

"Wow 10:30," Michael was already dressed and playing League of Legends at his desk. "Sleep ok?"

"Yeah, fine." She rubbed her tangled hair.

"Dream about me?"

"Always." She thought about Jing 2.0 on the mountain overlooking the valley.

"Remember taking the Blu2?"

"Yep. But I don't think it works on me."

"So, it's safe."

"I didn't say that. Just I didn't feel anything different."

"Okay, well you can try again. Maybe White Claw acts as an antidote." They both laughed knowing that was not true.

"Maybe." And she disappeared into the bathroom to pee and do something with the rat's nest on her head.

———

Abby knew where they kept the Blu2 and swiped a vial. Jing watched her do it, and told Michael, who said, "Let it go; let's see what happens."

Over the next couple of weeks, Abby got hooked. She was visiting more and more, and each time, taking a little Blu2 from the supply. She increased the dosage and was having lucid dreams, each one magnificent, where she was going to exotic places with amazing people.

Michael confronted her about the pilfering after she had stolen the equivalent of ten doses in two weeks. "Abby. I know you've been swiping some Blu from the fridge. Are you taking it every night?"

She didn't deny it. "Yep. What do you want me to say? You're right. It's safe."

"No. I want you to stop taking it. It seems like you are using more and more, and we don't know what the limit is. I'm concerned you might be addicted. We've locked the fridge. No more Blu."

"Fine. I'm not addicted. I'm fine."

"Good. Well, no more."

"Once in a while?"

"Okay. But we control the supply. We're not drug dealers, *remember*?"

———

Abby sat in her one-bedroom apartment. *Only two vials left. Two good nights. Or one great night.* Tomorrow she didn't have class until two.

———

She met up with Michael the next day. "I'm out, no more stuff. Think I'll just stay off it for a while."

"Yeah, probably a good idea. Wanna go back to your place and fool around?"

"Sure. I've got some homework due later tonight, though."

At her apartment, Michael locked the door behind them and charged her, knocking her to the ground. She tried to fight back, but his face was a twisted metal shape with razor-sharp teeth, and he bit into her face. She blacked out.

When she awoke he was gone, and she was in her bed. *A dream?* She turned to get up, but her face was stuck to the pillowcase with dried blood. *Not a dream.* Her face started to bleed again as she peeled off the pillowcase and ran to the bathroom to inspect the damage: a set of puncture wounds in the shape of a bite. She searched the medicine cabinet but there were no Band-Aids. When she closed the mirrored cabinet door she expected to see Michael standing behind her, but he wasn't there.

Holding some toilet paper to her face, she checked behind the shower curtain: the shower was empty. The bedroom closet, empty. Hall closet, empty. *Might have some Band-Aids in the kitchen.* The front door was locked. She didn't find any Band-Aids in the kitchen, and the toilet paper was doing the trick.

She considered calling the police. *Had it even been Michael?* Why did she feel like it wasn't him? Like it was a robot him? It sounded impossible, but the bite marks weren't imaginary.

She laid down on the couch to think things through, and fell asleep. When she awoke, he was in her face; it was as if he was falling from the ceiling toward her. The menacing mechanized face fell into hers, and she was churned into a thousand pieces, screaming as her flesh was ripped from her cheeks. She had blood in her eyes, but it was blue. She passed out.

When she awoke, there was no blood. Her skin was cool. And she knew why. It was metal. And she fled the apartment. People paid no attention as she raced by them to the University Police at Hemphill and tenth. She burst into the lobby, but she found no police there. Only ten Michaels, who turned and stared at her, then pounced.

———

Abby woke up at 1 p.m. She didn't know what day it was. *Oh, yeah, the Blu2*. And she had class in an hour. *That was a really bad nightmare*. To be sure, she checked in the mirror and saw a distressed, disheveled nineteen-year-old who was not a robot and did not have bite marks. She remembered the details of the dream vividly, but it was definitely a dream.

She decided to skip class and called her lab mate Geoff to ask him to take notes. Then she gave Michael a call that went to voicemail. When she turned around, her heart skipped. He was there.

"You called?"

He attacked her; the metal teeth came out, and the cycle repeated as before. She was locked in a never-ending cycle of horror. She prayed that she'd come out of it, but cycled through a half dozen more times until she woke up in a hospital.

Everything was extremely white, and the smell was antiseptic. The nurse came in, the first non-Michael in what seemed like a week-long fevered dream. "What happened?"

"You were found in the hallway of your apartment complex passed out. You fought off some of the people who tried to help you. And the police brought you here."

A woman in a lab coat came in. "I'm Dr. Townsend. I've been monitoring your progress since you were brought in. Your toxicology report and rape kit came back negative, but you've had a manic episode. Do you have any idea what might have caused it?"

Abby was about to say, "Blu2," when she saw Michael in the doorway and started screaming, "No! No! No!"

The nurse gave her a sedative while Dr. Townsend ushered Michael and Jing into the hall, telling them to try back later.

When Abby awoke, Dr. Townsend was there to ask her again if she knew what was affecting her. Though she knew Michael and the boys might get into trouble, she confessed to taking too much Blu2. Dr. Townsend, unfamiliar with Blu, or its sequel, listened to Abby's story, and then suggested voluntary admission to the Somerset Behavioral Health Hospital for further observation and Abby agreed it was her best option.

————

Abby entered the lobby, cautiously looking around, scared to be on her own again.

"Ma'am? Ma'am? Are you here to see a patient?"

"No, I... think I need to be admitted."

"Are you Abby Richardson?"

"Yes."

"We've been expecting you. Please wait a moment, and I'll have someone get you."

Abby glanced over her shoulder, scanning the waiting room. *He might be here already. But no one looks familiar.* An orderly escorted Abby past the locked door and down a series of halls, which seemed to her like a maze, to a white room, simply furnished with a high window. A TV was mounted on the wall, and a black remote sat on the white bed.

"This is your room," said the orderly, whose nametag, "Michael," almost set Abby off, but she kept it together. He checked his notes, "Mmmm... Dr. Baker... will be here soon. Please feel free to rest or watch TV. Would you like some water?"

"Yes, please."

"I'll be right back." He locked the door, more for Abby than himself, and left.

———

Abby awoke, and she was back in her apartment. She got out of bed not knowing what to think anymore. Headed to the bathroom. And Michael was there.

Dr. Baker and two orderlies struggled to get her sedated as she thrashed unconsciously in the white room.

———

Michael and Jing badged in. After graduation, they were hired by SinaFarm to create a safer Blu2, which had never officially existed. There was no chemical cure for reversing the effects of Blu overdose, or they would have worked on that instead. Blu2 was the only path forward. They owed it to Abby.

Michael: 45

I had no sight or sound, but I could remember the day I got married, the smile on my wife's brilliantly white teeth, and the way she had her hair done in those soft ringlets I had never seen before or since. My children were there, even though they had not yet been born. It was the most wonderful dream and then it faded away....

Bjorn: 35

All of a sudden everything is dark, but I feel like I'm going to throw up. I feel dizzy, like my brain is spinning inside my head. It's going around and around, and I can't make it stop. The inertia feels like it's pinned to one side of my head, and the other side of my skull is empty. I can't open my eyes, and I can't feel my body. I think I might be dying.

Catherine: 34

Arghhh. It's the loudest noise imaginable! My head's going to explode. I can't see anything but scattered flashes of light and that unbelievable loudness and pressure! Like an endless train driving through my skull with its horn blasting. I'm praying someone will kill me, or I will black out, but it's been going on for minutes. I can't feel pain, just unbearable loudness. It's so loud I want to die.

Jenny: 14

My... Jenny... fire... what? what? where are? They... what? Who? Brother... I fell off the swing... Our cat...he's missing! Fire! where am I... ahggg, the devil! she tore it up! My period, no, not... today! Fire! I can't breathe... where? Why? Why? Why? why why....

Joe: 52

"Well, Dan, we just got the results back from the coroner, it looks like the pilot, Michael Goedert, may have died from sudden myocardial infarction—a heart attack. The three passengers likely died instantly as the plane hit the mountainside. Luckily, they didn't feel any pain."

FIRE ESCAPE

I travel a lot for work, and it's a struggle dealing with all of my hotel phobias. You see, when you've gone to as many places as I've been, you're bound to run into some predicaments over time that you don't want to re-encounter.

Like once I got into bed and it was wet under the covers, so now I always pat the sheets, checking for dampness. I survey everything for general cleanliness using a black light and a green laser light. I bring my own toiletries; I verify the inside lock works, and I always check the fire escape plan.

A few years ago, at a regional hotel in Cambodia, the fire alarm malfunctioned, and I wandered the hall trying to find the exit. A maid, who was going about her work, ignoring the clanging sound, showed me the egress, marked in Khmer. So, when I got to my hotel room in Malawi the first thing I checked, on the back of the door, was the fire escape plan. It was straightforward – an exit at each of the corners of the rectangular building.

I was pleased with the room – it passed all my cleanliness tests and even had safety-sealed toiletries. After a dinner of nsima and chicken stew in the restaurant, I returned to my room to phone my family and read.

I had dozed off, on top of the bed, fully clothed, when the siren went off. I calmly got up, grabbed my laptop, and made my way out into the smoke-filled hall. It was definitely not a false alarm.

Since I had done my homework, I remembered exits at both ends of the hall, and followed the corridor on my left to the end. At the door, a lady was coming out as I was trying to go in. I asked her if there was fire in the stairwell, and she said, "No, this is my room. The exit is down at the other end," and pointed to the way from which I had just come.

I was upset the diagram was off, but I said, "Sorry, c'mon," and we made our way back to the other exit. The woman dropped to the floor where the air was less smoky, and I followed suit, moving as fast as possible. Personally, I would have just held my breath and run to the end, but I had this lady with me, so we did it her way.

When we got to the opposite corner, the door had a number on it, and a man and woman came out. Shouting above the alarm, the man said the exit was down the other way where the first woman's room was. I told them, "No!" And motioning to the woman on the floor I said, "She came out of that door. Our signs say your door's an exit."

He went back in his room and looked at the sign, and hastily reported back. "It says it's an exit, but it's not! It's our room."

"Well, let's try that one," and I pointed down the perpendicular hall.

"Drop to the ground," advised the woman, who I later learned was Mavis. "Less smoke." And like me, the man and the lady with him joined us on the carpet without questioning it.

Apparently, everyone was confused about the exits, including four people crawling toward us from the third corner. "It's just a room down there. No exit."

"Same here!"

One of the men stood up and ushered us into his suite. "Everyone in here; we'll block the smoke and call for help."

So the eight of us filed in and congregated around the fire escape plan on the back of the door, which looked exactly like the one on the back of my door.

"I'll be damned," said Mavis, "your map *does* show an exit where my room is. What the hell?"

Mark and Amy, from the second room, opened the window to the side yard and saw people filing out onto the grounds.

"Help!" Amy shouted at the people below, who were making "walk around" gestures up at us.

Martin, whose room it was, was wetting towels for the base of the door to try to keep smoke out. Another guy, Andy, who was staying directly across the hall, offered to see if there were any instructions from the courtyard. He was back in less than a minute, saying the whole courtyard was on fire, and we needed to stick to the outside rooms.

I popped my head out the window, scanning the facade for any other guests in our same position, but it seemed like everyone was clear but us.

Jill and Frederika, who were in the last group with Martin and Andy, were sitting upright in the bed. I think Jill was having a panic attack and Frederika was trying to calm her down.

Andy volunteered to go back out and try the fourth corner. After five minutes he hadn't returned, nor was he safe below. We worried he may have gotten too much smoke and passed out.

Mark was on the phone with the manager who said to use the exit in the corner. He was yelling back at her saying his room was "...*in the bloody corner!*"

The room was getting hot, and not just because the AC had swapped places with the warm, dry Malawi air. I feared the flames were surrounding us.

That's when the bed, along with Jill and Frederika, crashed through the floor into the room below. The shock of the floor giving way was superseded by horrific screams as the fire engulfed them. Their shrieking is something I'll never forget, and it brings tears to my eyes even today.

Now that the center of our room was compromised, it would be only a matter of time until the rest of it failed.

Mark and Amy, at the window, were separated from me, Martin, and Mavis by the fiery chasm, but we managed to get them across the credenza along the wall. So now the five of us were trapped in the bathroom and entryway, and the door was red hot. We were sure we were going to die.

After sweating out ten long minutes, we heard loud voices in the hall, and we started shouting back. An axe came through the door, and Martin opened it to save them the trouble, burning his palm on the handle.

Men in firefighter uniforms ushered us through what I believed to be an inside room on the corner of the hallway. We fled down the concrete steps and, at the next level, crossed to an outside corner room, which was the marked exit to the ground floor. Paramedics met us with a single oxygen tank and mask that we passed around, grateful to be alive.

In the aftermath, the hotel company conceded the exit maps were not correct for the fifth floor, which had been a late add-on with special corner suites. So, the four exits were on the inside corners of the hallways. Good to know. Not that it matters anymore. The hotel burned to the ground.

We also confirmed that Andy perished en route to the fourth exit, which was obviously not where we thought it would be.

After being released by the paramedics, I bought replacement clothes and checked into another place down the street. Amazingly, I was exhausted enough that I somehow was able to sleep, but only after walking all seven exit routes of the new building, *twice*.

THE BLEEDING CHURCH OF SAN MIGUEL DE LOS LLANOS

As our expedition made its way across the Argentinian-Paraguayan border, at the confluence of the Paraná and Paraguay Rivers, we began the task of surveying and mapping the department of Ñeembucú.

Our guide, a native of the region, raved about visiting the nearby town of San Miguel de Los Llanos and the *iglesia sangrante,* or "bleeding church."

Southern Paraguay, colonized by the Jesuit order in the 16th century, is dotted with many small, local churches worth investigating for their interesting architecture and histories. However, we deemed that the church's reputation as a bleeding church was nothing more than folklore.

On the third week, as we worked our way north, toward Pilar, our guide became fanatical, imploring us to visit the church, explaining that San Miguel de Los Llanos was only a day's hike from our current position. Although we were on a strict timetable, two companions and I decided to accompany him to experience the famous village.

The rudimentary maps we were tasked with perfecting showed no such town as San Miguel de Los Llanos, but that was not uncommon. Our guide was an expert in the indigenous tribes and topography of the region. If he said the place existed, it most likely did.

As if drawn by a strong magnet, he paced us through dense forestation and dry valleys until we saw a settlement rise out of the plain, and we reached a wide road, lined with stables and fruit carts.

One could not mistake the Bleeding Church, looming at the end of the main thoroughfare, where a much narrower road crossed perpendicularly. Erected out of red brick, likely imported by European colonizers, it contrasted with the grayish-tan adobe dwellings of the town. Even if it didn't physically bleed, the church was the color of oxygenated blood, a bright scarlet, and the moniker was fitting.

The villagers were hospitable, and we expressed our thanks in gestures. We also offered supplies, which was customary, and, in some towns, necessary to guarantee security. In San Miguel de Los Llanos it was only the former as we felt no threat of harm from the peaceful and religious people.

All night, the wind roared across the plains. The sturdy huts were built to withstand the weather, but come morning, we were roused by commotion on the street. Our hosts informed us that the church was "bleeding."

As we approached, we perceived the exterior walls to be streaked with dark red rivulets, which hadn't been there the day before. I surmised the high winds during the night carried a small rainstorm, which deposited water on the church's roof that now ran down the façade because there were no gutters on the rood, and no downspouts. Although the ground was not wet, the dry desert roads could have easily and quickly absorbed a light shower.

Villagers lined the church's exterior, touching the crimson streaks and genuflecting. Our guide motioned for me to join him, saying, "*Sangre*," "The Blood!" and showed me how the substance glistened on his fingertips. He repeatedly did this, making the sign of the cross on his forehead over and over to receive the nearly unlimited blessings the blood entitled him to.

Still skeptical, I approached the wall and rubbed my finger down the length of a particularly dark line that caught my eye. I expected to feel a gritty, water-based texture from the erosion of the brick, but it was viscous. *Sticky....*

Instinctively, I smelled my fingers and picked up a metallic scent. I dared to taste it and was eyed-up suspiciously by more than one villager, perhaps fearing I had cannibalistic tendencies. It tasted briny. *Maybe it was just water and dust.*

Our guide and the others continued to sanctify themselves while my companions declined to touch the streaks, concluding it was "an interesting phenomenon" and "not blood."

Not pleased with my lack of participation, our guide attempted to make the sign of the cross on my forehead, which I permitted. My companions refused to be marked as such, and, instead, ordered him to pack our things so we could return to our encampment by evening.

On our way out of town, I thanked our guide for the excursion, happy to have enjoyed a cultural nuance as a break from the tedium of surveying. I asked him if the church "bled" frequently. He replied that we experienced a very special day, indeed, as the phenomenon only happened once every few years. This revelation was not consistent with my rainfall theory, as the region is temperate with regular precipitation.

Less than an hour from our base camp, natives accosted our party. Despite a generous offer to take our remaining supplies and leave in peace, they attacked my two traveling companions with crude machetes, mortally wounding one and cutting deep into the forearm of the other. Though we applied a tourniquet, he succumbed to his injury a week later.

Our guide took me aside and claimed that the blood from the church protected us from the onslaught, while the non-believers were targeted. I was about to disagree, to tell him I was also a non-believer, but I carefully reconsidered, for his sake, and thanked him for my "blessing." And in the time it took me to think about how much I didn't believe, I realized how much I did.

SHADOW OF A DOUBT

Mötley Crüe's song "Shout at the Devil" was blaring over the car stereo as we hauled ass at breakneck speed. My best friend Patrick (we called him Packy) and I were in his '72 Rally Nova, heading on Forest Drive near Dead Man's Curve at a terrifying seventy-five miles per hour. I ripped into him. "Slow down, dude! You're going way too fast!" and I gripped the "Oh Shit" handle above the passenger window.

"Chill out; you're afraid of your own shadow," and he laughed as he pushed it up to eighty.

Nearing the curve, he reduced his speed to sixty, which was still about forty over the limit and five over his previous record, his courage coming from the recent purchase of a couple of fat P265 tires. I was terrified we weren't going to make it, and we'd roll the car down the embankment at the apex of the turn.

The bend itself was shrouded in sunlight that was beaming through the trees at an odd angle and making everything white. I was praying for no oncoming cars. Other motorists were few and far between on this road, and it would be highly unlikely to encounter one.

I half-closed my eyes, both from the sun and the fear, as we approached the seventy-degree unbanked turn, and, as we crested around the cairn at the edge, the tires held. As if propelled by a slingshot, Packy accelerated to the chant of "six-tee-four – six-tee-four" against the background of Mick Mars' guitar solo.

We finished the drive through the rest of the highland at a respectable seventy to ninety miles per hour, with easy curves and gentle slopes, getting to the lodge just before sunset.

Mira and Jeannette were already there: Mira's Ford Escort was out front. They had probably come in after her Friday morning class and driven through Jamestown to pick up some groceries. We were looking for some weekend fun: drinking, sex, swimming in the lake, and more sex. Having been friends before we started dating each other, we hoped it wouldn't become complicated, and so far, it hadn't.

Mira ran over and launched her 108-pound frame into my arms as we came through the door. She had clearly gotten a head start on me from her sunshiny disposition and the Bartles & Jaymes pack that was three-quarters empty behind her on the bar.

Packy and I didn't drink when we raced the Nova – we had better sense than that. But, come to think of it, it was likely more out of respect for the car than for either of our lives. I'd driven Mira's Escort drunk dozens of times.

The weekend was a blast: no thoughts of school or work, and we didn't want it to end. We didn't leave the cabin until four, which would put us back in town by dusk, and we'd be through the forest well before then.

Mira and Jeanette went back through Jamestown: it was quicker, but a lot less fun than the forest drive, so we hugged goodbyes, and split at the "Y" about three miles from the cabins. Packy popped in some Def Leppard as I hit the accelerator.

The Nova was Packy's, but he let me drive it on the open roads. Outside the forest's edge, we pulled over and swapped. He wanted to take it back around Dead Man's, this time with the left turn. We always took that turn fast, never knowing if another car or deer was coming the other way; we believed the statistics were always in our favor.

As we neared the curve, with AC/DC's "Back in Black" on the cassette player, I was nervous, even though the tires had been solid on the last pass. At least the approach was away from the sun this time, so it was easier to see.

Packy was already hitting eighty at fifty yards out. This time I didn't close my eyes at all, but still grabbed the "Oh Shit" handle as he got to eighty-five. And then, fifty feet out, Packy saw something in the road. He swerved into the rock wall on the left. The front end of the car crunched as we careened directly across the road to the right and everything went black.

I woke up and everything was still black. But this was because it was now night. We were stopped, and I immediately knew we had been in a wreck.

"Back in Black" was still playing at a thousand decibels, and I reached over and shut it off. It was like no time had passed, but definitely, a lot had. I'm sure the cassette had flipped multiple times.

I tried to get my bearings. A large tree was laying across the hood, and my seatbelt was excruciatingly tight through my chest. So I unbuckled it and fell forward into the dash and window.

The front of the Nova was down, and we were up against a tree.

Packy was slumped against the steering wheel. I was sure if the car fell on its side we would be hurt further, so I was cautious as I reached over and gently shook him. He looked in bad shape, and I feared he was dead. I still couldn't tell in the darkness if he was breathing, and I couldn't see his face.

I switched on the dome light, which blinded me for a second, then checked his wrist for a pulse. I couldn't find one. So I grabbed him by the back of his hair and turned him toward me yelling, "Pack!" and it startled me that his eyes were open. He had the most horrified look on his face. Utter despair. His mouth was agape as if he saw the face of death moments before it arrived.

I shoved his head away from me, retreating to my side of the car. The engine was no longer running, but the dome light and my AC/DC wake-up alarm both indicated we still had a strong battery. I hit the hazard button as a signal in case another motorist could see the rear lights, and tried to figure out how to escape.

Carefully, I unlatched the door and slowly creaked it open. The cool night felt inviting. Eager to replace the stagnant air in the car, I pushed it open a little too fast, and it pulled from my grasp. I braced for impact, sure the inertia of the heavy door falling would tip us over.

But the car didn't fall. Now I was confident I could jump free without it falling on me, however, I couldn't see a landing spot. For all I knew I'd be rolling down a hill to my death, if I wasn't first speared by a branch sticking out of the ground.

Then, from the corner of my eye, I saw movement: likely my shadow cast by the dome light, but when I turned, it had gone. I tried to move between the light and the tree to confirm, but I couldn't place my head in the right spot. When I reached out with my hand, its shadow moved against the tree. Then, a second, larger hand reached across the trunk.

Probably concussed, seeing things that weren't there. I sensed several other movements—unclear as to their source—in my peripheral vision. They moved even when I was still. *Animals? Maybe I would be safer in the car with Packy than trying to strike it out at night on my own.*

I reached down to pull the door shut and wait for help. It might be a while, but when we didn't show up the next day, they'd look for us. I grabbed the "Oh Shit" handle and cantilevered out to grab the door when I fell out of the seat. And I pulled the car over with me.

By the grace of God, I landed softly; hanging from the handle had lessened the drop, and the open door and the cabin fell around me, the door propping up the car on its side. I slid out of the way and scrambled up the hill before the car could roll any further, but it never did.

Up on the roadside, with the car about fifteen feet below me, I was roughly at the apex of Dead Man's Curve. Packy was too young to have had a dying wish list, but being in the Nova at Dead Man's Curve when he cashed out would probably have been near the top.

I was unofficially still in shock. I had not mourned the death of my closest friend and was clueless what to do next.

The hazard lights' glow was barely perceptible. No one would ever have seen them if they were driving by.

I decided to walk toward the nearest town, Fallstaff, which was on the far side of the forest; I guessed about six miles from Dead Man's Curve.

The high moon cast patches of moonlight onto the surface of the road. I moved from light to light, still catching movement on the neighboring trees, though my shadow was below me, where it should be.

No cars came by, as suspected, and I resigned myself to walking the entire distance. As I neared the edge of the forest, I could make out the lights of Fallstaff, but the only source of illumination there was the moon, now at an angle, casting a faint and small shadow of me to the left.

When I reached the town, I had no idea where to go, but the bright lights of a twenty-four-hour laundromat caught my eye. A guy about my age was doing middle-of-the-night laundry, and I begged him to help.

I told him we had been in a car wreck in the forest, and my friend was dead, which now seems like oversharing, but I wasn't thinking straight at that point. He mumbled something like he didn't want to get involved, but threw me a quarter to use the pay phone and call the cops.

While I waited outside, my shadows danced everywhere, projected from the various points of light coming from inside the laundromat and its sign. And there was still something disconcerting with them. They seemed slightly out of sync with my movements, like they were copying me, but a tenth of a second too late.

Starting to feel a little creeped out again, I went back inside the laundromat to wait. I debated calling the girls, but I didn't know what to say about Packy.

One cop arrived, which I guessed was all they were staffed with at two in the morning. Officer John Franks took my initial statement and asked me to ride out with him to the scene.

I told Franks I had awakened upright against the tree and discovered Packy, *Patrick,* was dead. I also told him that I believed Packy had seen something or someone in the street right before he swerved. I almost mentioned the strange shadows and the creatures in the forest, but I checked myself before sounding full-on crazy.

Franks made a point to reinforce that the bend was safe at the posted speed limit, implying we might have been racing. "Never had anyone go off the road there," he said. Nevertheless, he agreed to check for reports of vagrants in the area and radioed the dispatch for an ambulance and a wrecker.

In a few minutes, we were back at the scene. He parked a good hundred feet back from the curve and put on all his lights, including his high beams and that special floodlight cops have on the side of their car. I was now hyper-aware of my shadow being cast in all directions by the whirling and bright lights. There were so many of me, even more than there should have been, and all acting erratically, not in sync with my movements.

I asked Franks if he had the same sensation, and to him everything seemed normal. He looked at me somewhat curiously, but then changed his disposition and told me,

"You've been through some trauma, Mike. If this is too much, you can wait in the car, and I'll go check it out."

I told him I'd be alright. I owed it to Packy to be there.

Franks carried a single flashlight: a good one that illuminated the whole road. He shone it down the embankment, and I pointed out the car, still on its side with the door bracing it.

Franks indicated we would wait for the ambulance and wrecker and not do anything ourselves. I agreed, and we walked back to the cruiser. As we got closer, the shadows were dancing again. I closed my eyes but for a crack to keep pace with the officer, and got back in the vehicle, sweating bullets. Franks went back out and lit flares all along the road, ...*to conjure up as many shadows as possible*, I thought.

Within a half-hour, an ambulance arrived from Ashville and parked just past the curve, facing toward us with its own dazzling light show. Franks asked if I was okay to visit the scene again, and I made my way through the prismatic lights, catching my shadow out of every corner of my eyes. I was like a bumblebee, seeing hundreds of images simultaneously, and yet none of them represented the true me. They were impostor shadows, doing their own thing, and taunting me with their freedom.

The EMTs pulled Packy from the wreck, strapped his lifeless body to a board, drew it up the slope, and loaded him in the back of the ambulance. An EMT named Annie looked at my injuries and asked me if I wanted a ride to the hospital. I turned her down but should have accepted.

The tow truck showed up, and now the forest was brighter than during the day. My shadows retreated into the surrounding vegetation. Not gone, but lurking. I might have been happier keeping an eye on them.

The Nova was righted and pulled from the ravine, and they let me get my bag out of the trunk. I left Packy's stuff there. He wouldn't be needing it.

I rode back to town with Franks as daylight approached.

As the sun shone through the windshield, I looked behind me, and there it was, my shadow again, just sitting in the backseat where it should be. *Yesterday afternoon… it would have been in front of me. Had Packy seen my shadow as the sun cut behind us through the trees fifty feet from Dead Man's Curve? Or had I seen it?*

Suddenly, I was hit by guilt. Tears welled in my eyes, and my face got hot. Like somehow I had something to do with the accident. Franks asked if I was okay, and told me to "…let it out."

It may have been the product of a guilty mind, but at that moment I thought I had seen it. Right against the rock, *or was it closer? Like on the road? It could have been. Did I not recognize my own shadow? Did I think it was another person? Did I reach over and push the steering wheel to avoid it?*

John always preferred plucking out his nose hair to trimming it.

He'd check to make sure no one was watching, grab the extra-long hair between his thumb and middle finger, close his eyes and tense all the muscles in his face to brace for the pain, and then with one swift motion, pull the offender from its roots. He'd examine it to see if it was black or gray – the gray ones were the thickest and hardest to pull out. *A satisfying achievement.* Then he'd discard it on the ground with never a thought of it again.

One day, as John sat in his office, with a view of the Monongahela River and the WESA-FM tower on Mount Washington, he detected a rogue hair creeping down toward his upper lip, one of those "wild hairs" that seem to grow two inches in a day.

He grabbed it, anticipating success, because he couldn't get such a good grip on it. But as he made the scrunched-up face and pulled, it never snapped at the base. He opened his eyes, thinking it still somehow slipped from his grasp, but there it was, still pinched, but now a foot long and still embedded in his nose.

John was stunned. He walked across the office to where he had a sales award with shiny metal sides and inspected. Sure enough, the now-foot-long hair was still intact and hanging out toward the ground.

"What the…," he thought, but never finished the sentence. Instead, he grabbed the hair again, very close to his nose, and gave it a test tug. To his surprise, the hair pulled easily but still did not come out of the socket.

At this point, John couldn't tell if he was stretching the hair, or if there was more inside him, but as absurd as it sounded in his mind, he still felt it was more reasonably the latter. So, he pulled a little bit more out, and a little more. Soon the hair was long enough that it hung to his knees.

He didn't know what to do. Calling in his administrative assistant would be a mistake, *that girl gossiped like nobody else.* He decided to cut the hair and deal with it at home.

He didn't have any scissors in his office, but he had a cigar cutter, which worked fine. He was just done cutting it when his boss Frank knocked and came in. Frank wanted to chit-chat about a new potential merger, so it wasn't a short discussion, and all the while the cigar cutter and four-foot-long hair were in John's lap.

At the end, Frank mentioned to John that he had an unusually long nose hair that needed to be clipped. John thanked him for the observation, and after Frank finally left, John gathered up his briefcase and the hair and drove to his house in nearby Shadyside.

His wife Janice wasn't at home, which gave John time to investigate this new situation. In the bathroom, he found the newly clipped hair still hanging out about two inches, which was the closest he could get with the cigar cutter. He gave it a slight tug and as expected, the hair pulled out a little more.

John gave it a long pull, all the way to arm's length, and the hair just kept coming out. He started to panic and pulled it out in a hand-over-hand motion until he had made a considerable pile.

Janice called up to John, having seen his car in the driveway, and he clipped it off with a fingernail clipper.

John asked her to come upstairs and sit on the bed next to him, where he revealed his strange malady. She was in disbelief until he showed her the sixteen-foot-long hair he had just cut.

"Now hold still, let me see this...," she directed as she delicately grabbed the tip of the hair with her manicured nails, tickling the inside of John's nose. She pulled hard (like he hadn't tried that before), and ended up with a two-foot-long hair which she dropped, shrieking.

"It never ends," John said. And then demonstrated hand over hand how he could keep pulling on it forever.

"Can you feel it inside you?" asked Janice, who had calmed down.

"No. It's like it's coming from another dimension. There's no way I coulda had twenty feet of hair in my nose and I wouldn't know it."

Janice looked it up on the internet, but there were no reports of unending hairs of any type. "I think you're just going to have to live with it, Johnny...; maybe you can go on a talk show and make some money with it."

"It's not a talent, Janice; it's a curse." John was furious. "I don't want anyone to ever know about this. Got it?"

Janice had never seen this side of him but realized that deep down he was just scared. "John, dear, please just trim it like a normal person. It's probably 'cause you yank those things out all the time; it's getting back at you."

No matter how far-fetched that sounded, it was the only explanation that made sense. So, John went online and bought a nose hair trimmer, which arrived the next day. He was apprehensive to use it, but afterward, he no longer felt like he was tempted to pull on the hair. He couldn't get his fat fingers that far up there anyway.

John started using the trimmer religiously and broke his nose-hair-pulling habit for good. Well, almost. Sometimes, when Janice is out with the girls, he'll borrow her tweezers and tug on the hairs in his nose, ever so slightly, until he finds that one, and he'll pull out about thirty feet of hair because he can.

REFUSAL

Felipe Herrera was like any other young Catholic boy growing up in Mexico. He went to mass with his family every Sunday, said prayers before bed and eating, and even met his first girlfriend in confirmation class. They were only fourteen, but somehow Felipe knew she was his forever partner. The feeling was mutual, and they continued to invite each other to social events. Carmen asked him to be the main *chambelon* at her *quinceañera* the following March, and he was overjoyed. He himself would be fifteen only a few weeks later and understood it was a big step for her, and for them.

Their town of Culebra, on the outskirts of Mexico City, was no stranger to violence. Multiple gangs claimed the territory as their own, and the residents kept their heads down, trying to avoid the eye of whoever was in charge, or next in charge.

Carmen's dad, Jaime, was a local businessman with a small group of fruit stands, constantly being fleeced by the cartels for protection money. He never fought back and was an easy target. Frutería Hernández didn't make a lot of profit as it was, so when Cartel Velasco upped his *tributo* from 3000 to 5000 pesos a week, Jaime was underwater.

Even then, Jaime was determined to give his only daughter the *quinceañera* celebration she deserved. Local families donated food and decorations to make the central warehouse sparkle. All the fruit was pushed to the borders of the large central room and a dance floor was created under pink and purple crepe paper streamers.

Carmen, dressed in a long, fluffy, chiffon dress appeared like a Disney princess. Felipe had never seen her with makeup before; it wasn't her normal style, and he thought she looked eighteen, or even twenty! As they danced the waltz they had been rehearsing for a month, it felt natural and light. Everyone remarked about what a beautiful young couple they made.

The festivities went all night, and by early morning, Carmen had her shoes off and was dressed comfortably in a small pink dress that hovered just above her knees.

Most of the partygoers had returned home to rest from the night of festivities when Raul Velasco appeared in the doorway to the warehouse with five of his gang. He called out to Jaime, "You got so much money for this nice party? You can now pay 10,000 pesos a week."

The remaining guests tried to not make eye contact, but Carmen was enraged and charged up to Raul. "How dare you come in here, uninvited, to my party. Leave! Now!"

Raul picked up an apple, bit into it once then threw it on the ground, looking at Jaime, but pointing at Carmen. "So feisty, this one. Are you sure she's yours, Señor Hernández?"

Then he walked toward Carmen addressing her in a quiet tone, "Ah, *chiquita*, you see…, I was not aware that my employee here, was spending our money in this way." He looked over to Jaime and then slapped Carmen across the face, knocking her to the ground.

Jaime charged Raul, but the click of guns from Raul's team stopped him. Raul shouted at both of them, "I'm the boss!" pointing vigorously to his chest. "Now, it's 20,000!"

and he walked over to one of his gunmen, grabbed the automatic rifle and started shooting all the fruit against the right wall. "20,000. One week." And he left.

Jaime and Felipe rushed over to see if Carmen was alright, but she was already getting up and ready to head out the door after the gangsters in her bare feet. They had to hold her back. "It's only money, *mi'ija*," explained Jaime. He managed to scrounge up the tribute, but over the following weeks, he was unable to keep up with the cartel's demands.

One day, Felipe hadn't heard from Carmen. He went to her house and the police were there. A distraught Señora Hernández revealed that her baby girl had been abducted. Within the next few days, Carmen was gone forever, their precious princess, now an angel with the Lord.

But Felipe wondered what kind of god would take such an innocent and allow the unjust to live. He told God that since He had made His choice, Felipe would also. He would refuse God.

He stopped going to church and joined the occult. He tattooed his body from head to toe with pagan symbols and atheistic slogans. He joined a gang, and murdered, and thieved. He kept a diary of his transgressions against the Ten Commandments to ensure he consistently broke them. It became a personal war with God. He'd shake his fist at the heavens, saying, "You had no right!" In doing all this, he never doubted the existence of God; no, it was just that he wanted to defy him in a volume equal to, or more than, the way he felt betrayed. He knew that he would go to Hell and never see Carmen again, for she was certainly in Heaven. But he could not bring himself to forgive God.

So, when he passed, at the hands of another good man, like Jaime Hernández, he expected to wake up in the fiery pits of Hell. Instead, he was inside the gates of Heaven. And there was Carmen, only three feet away. And he shouted out, "I have defiled your name again and again! Why have you brought me here?"

And God replied, "It is your choice as my creation to refuse me, but I will not refuse you, my child." And He locked Felipe in a clear box not far from Carmen, where he lived 1000 years for each transgression God deemed grievous. Over two million years, Felipe softened – his tattoos and hate fading and his love for Carmen growing.

And God knew this would happen, for God is all-knowing and has used many millions of boxes.

And when Felipe got out it was just the right amount of time to start anew, and he and Carmen lived together in heavenly bliss for the rest of eternity.

THINK IT THROUGH

I knew I wasn't thinking straight, but I didn't care. As I sat in my Ford Bronco at the lookout, the headlights illuminating the empty space ahead all I wanted was for the pain to be over.

Two hundred feet straight down should be enough to do the job.

I gunned the engine, and the wheels spun trying to find traction on the hardpan. When they finally caught, instead of vaulting over the lip, I weakly tipped over the edge and drove down the side of the cliff. I was upright until twenty feet from the bottom where the car hit an outcropping and flipped forward, landing on its front. I smashed through the steering wheel into the windshield, hoping it wasn't too little, too late.

It was. I woke up, disoriented. And angry. *Couldn't even do this right.* The pain in my left arm was excruciating, and my palm was facing away from me in a way I'd never seen before. My elbow was pinned inside of the crushed windshield frame. I wasn't going anywhere.

My right arm had disappeared through a hole in the dash. I tried to pull it out, but there were jagged plastic pieces that had pushed in with it. Pulling out against those caused them to slice into my forearm, but I eventually worked it free. With no way to bandage it, I just watched it bleed for a minute or so until I was distracted by the smell of blood from my head wound. No longer running, but not dried, I felt its sticky residue caked around my eye and down my cheek.

I looked down toward the rearview mirror to check it out, but the mirror had gone with the windshield. I spotted it a few yards away on the desert floor.

No one had arrived to help me yet. As it was dawn, I knew it had already been six hours. *If they did show up,* I thought ruefully, *I might just finally die... of embarrassment.* I could say it was an accident, but the forensics team would know better. I remembered spinning my wheels in the sand like a moron before barely going over the edge.

The road near the lookout was well traveled, but it wasn't tourist season, and there were plenty of prettier and better-marked lookouts all along the road. It's why I had chosen this one. At that point I didn't know if I wanted to be found.

The pain was also still in my heart as I recalled the events of the previous evening: Mr. Koutous' lackeys torturing my wife and daughter to death to send a message.

Of course, I'd wanted revenge, but despair for the loss of my loves drove me in a different direction. *If they wanted the information, they were never going to get it. They had lost their only leverage and now I was taking it to my grave,* or so I thought.

The Arizona sun was already starting to come up, with its oppressive heat, and at the car's angle, it was heating up the air around me. The glint off the rearview mirror acted as a magnifying glass reflecting the sun straight into my eyes.

Turning away, I saw the Gila monster. It was at least ten feet away, plodding through the sand in my general direction, not at me, but close enough that I felt threatened. I looked around for something to defend myself with, and I found the Jim Beam bottle, which was intact and within reach.

I remembered drinking most of it the night before, to wipe away the grief and give me the courage to drive off the cliff, but, sadly, not the smarts to do it properly. At that moment I was sober and dehydrated. I thought about breaking on the bottle against the dash to use as a weapon, but I figured I might need it later to wet my whistle. It might be the only liquid I'd have for a while.

I had heard Gila monster bites were venomous and painful, and I prayed he'd find another critter to snack on. But the big lizard crept closer and closer, curious to see what I was about.

My dislocated hand was the closest part of my body to the ground, and he spotted it. Now, he was only a few feet away. He started to stare intently at it. I couldn't so much as wiggle my fingers to scare him away. With my working hand I took my keys out of the ignition and threw them at the beast to get him to go. They hit the ground only a couple of inches from him, but he was unfazed, in a trance looking at my delicious, meaty hand.

And then he lurched at it and bit down.

I thought it was going to be life-changing pain, but I didn't feel a thing as he proceeded to bite off huge chunks of my hand as if he'd never been fed before.

As I watched in disbelief, I could only reason that the nerves had been severed inside the car frame. Once he had detached a sufficiently large portion of my hand, he scurried off, taking it with him.

It didn't bleed, which was also a bad sign. I reasoned the window frame must have been clamped down like a tourniquet on my forearm.

I thought about reinserting my right arm back into the jagged dashboard and scraping it until I bled to death, but if this colossal failure of a suicide attempt had taught me anything, it was that I was bad at it. I realized I'd probably just end up with two dead arms.

I began to change my drive away from death and toward a new purpose in life: to avenge my family. Even if I died going after Koutous, I'd be no worse off than I was in that moment.

Deciding to wait it out, I took a few sips of JB and fell asleep. And awoke to excruciating pain in my cheek.

I thought a coyote or mountain lion had attacked me, but it was a huge fucking bird with a razor-sharp beak. Protecting my face as best I could, I flailed at it, but it just kept attacking me from its perch on the passenger seat.

I attempted to club it with the bottle, but it grabbed my arm with its talons and tore off my ear with its beak. As it clung to me, I started scraping it against the remaining glass jutting out from around the edge of the windshield. We fought for several minutes until eventually he died, his claws sunk deep into the old wounds of my forearm. My adrenaline finally exhausted, I couldn't even pry his carcass off.

Touching my destroyed face, I felt my jawbone. Not my jaw, but the actual bone itself, and my teeth. Not through my mouth, through the side.

I was sure now I would bleed out before anyone got there. As I started to pass out, I noticed a trail of ants going from my former left hand to the desert floor.

I woke up on a stretcher with a helicopter sound in the near distance. I had a very tight wrap above my left elbow, a proper tourniquet, and they had immobilized my neck.

That's when I screamed as something stung my leg. I screamed out, "My leg!" And started to shake it, getting stung again and again. They eventually got my pants off to find a scorpion lodged in the pantleg. They treated the stings and loaded me into the chopper.

I'm sure they'll still be coming for me when I get out of this hospital. But that's okay with me. My body is getting better every day. Sure, I'll have one less arm, but I'll also have one *more* plan. Now I know what can happen when you don't think it through. And if a car crash, a Gila monster, a crazed bird, a scorpion, and embarrassment can't kill me, I'd like to see *them* try.

SWIMMIN' HOLE

I grew up in southern West Virginia, in the middle of nowhere. My family used to be miners, but that business went away, and times got really hard. But we stayed: this was where our ancestors lived, and they had less than we did.

My parents tried farming and crafts, and even though we was really poor, we survived. We was rarely hungry and had a good roof over our heads with a warm fireplace for those cold West Virginia nights.

In the summer, when we was out of school, I'd ride my bike about ten miles to the river and go swimmin' with my friends. But even better was I had my own swimmin' hole on our land. So, if I didn't feel like goin' all that way, I could just stay home and fish or swim until it was time for supper.

I remember, as a kid, the water in the swimmin' hole was pretty clear. I'd dive down and see the fish and the plants. But when I was about ten the swimmin' hole started to get cloudier. Papa said there was a trash dump north of us and those motherfuckers was pollutin' our land.

Sometimes things would wash down the stream and into our swimmin' hole. I didn't see a problem with it. Sometimes cool stuff would show up. I'd find a lot of really old bottles, and Papa would try to sell 'em in Lexington. We'd make almost a hundred every month from my bottles, and it made me proud to be helpin' the family; plus it was really cool.

I'd go to the swimmin' hole just about every day from April to September. As I got older I trained my body to withstand cold temperatures, so I could try to make money year-round, 'cept when the pond froze.

I never noticed when the water started turning greener. I guess when you go every day you don't notice small changes, but Momma said I was startin' to stink when I come back from the hole. I just showered with the hose before I went inside, and then everything was okay.

But one time I was divin' down, and it felt like something bit me in the eye. I hadn't seen any fish in some time and I figgered they just moved on. Anyway, it hurt really bad, so I went to grab my eye, and I ended up pushin' a needle into my eye. It was just barely in, but I pushed it in like another inch, and it hurt so bad I thought I was gonna drown. I pulled it out, got out, and ran home.

I was scared I'd never see from that eye again. Momma and Papa took me to the doctor. They bandaged it up and gave me medicine. It was really blurry for about five months, and I wasn't allowed to go back in the swimmin' hole. Papa said it was gettin' just too polluted and dangerous, and that we'd have to divert the stream from the trash dump and drain the hole.

I was really upset about losin' my only hobby. I started to do bad in school and act out. I fought with my old friends and also got beat up myself a bunch. I still wasn't allowed in the hole, but I was able to sneak away to it once in a while.

I traded my lunch with a kid at school for two weeks to get a pair of goggles which made seein' in the hole a lot better, but it still wasn't great. The water had got pretty green in the last year. I think it was because the outflow was blocked, and the trees would shed their leaves into the pool, and then when they rotted it would be green. But leaves aren't that big a deal, so I was okay with it.

When I was a senior in high school, a girl named Beccah, who was my age, moved into the farmhouse next to us. Not really close, maybe still a half mile away, but one day I heard her scream when I was swimmin' at the hole. I poked my head up and took off my goggles and she was at the edge of the hole pukin' and runnin' away. "So gross," she kept repeatin'. And then she passed out.

I didn't know what to do, so I gave her mouth-to-mouth resuscitation like we learned in school. I wasn't sure if I was doin' it right, but she woke up and gurgled out some breakfast and then started screamin' again. I backed away, not sure what her problem was. She started wipin' her mouth and cursin' at me. I was so confused, 'cause I felt like I had just saved her life.

She ran away, and I started to run after her, but she said, "Stay away you nasty freak." She was really cryin', and I could tell she was serious.

I went home and cleaned up and hoped to talk to her when she showed up at school, but she didn't come back until the followin' week. Even then she wouldn't make eye contact with me. She told people that I swam in shit at home, and that I ate shit, and I tried to kiss her, which was all lies.

The police showed up at our house and talked to my parents when I was at school. My dad gave me a beatin' for swimmin' in the hole and asked me if I raped that girl. I told them my side of the story, and I think they believed me, but I was grounded and suspended from school until they did an "inquiry."

They found out I was innocent. Beccah realized she wasn't raped, but she still said my rescue was "unwelcomed." We said she was trespassin', and both families agreed to let it drop.

The worst part is they cordoned off the swimmin' hole and the inbound stream all the way up to the dump with yellow tape. Guys in full-body white suits was there for about three months and eventually we had to move away to Kentucky. Dad said it was for work, but I know we lost the farm.

In Kentucky, I found another swimmin' hole, but this one had no treasure. There wasn't any needles in this one, but no rare bottles either. I didn't even need goggles.

I was still curious about our old house and my swimmin' hole, so when I was twenty-five I drove there. The gate was closed with a sign from the Department of Public Health saying the site was contaminated. I went over to Beccah's, and it was also closed, so I went back to our place and snuck onto our old land.

My swimmin' hole was covered in green slime and smelled just awful. But I stripped and dove in, just for old times' sake.

PROBE-LEM

Back in 2702, I was the leader of a scout mission to a small planet in the two-hundred and thirteenth sector of the fifth octant. While that sector was generally considered unremarkable, we had off-the-chart readings of biological life on a single planet. Our job was to journey there and to take samples, undetected.

The proper procedure was to enter the planet's atmosphere, cloaked: invisible to any known imaging device. We would target specimens with a photon blocker to induce a state of brain paralysis while remotely sampling tissue for DNA and other properties. The process was invasive, but unknown to the subject. We would send a robotic probe into the mouth or rectum of the creature and take samples from the inside. The biopsies would be returned to the central labs for recreation of the original subject, on which more tests would be conducted.

Most of the time we could accomplish this within hours of initial planetary contact. But in this 2702 case, as we scanned the planet for life, we came back with an astronomical variety of species – an impossible job for our team of four. We landed in an area with a diversity of fauna, far from anything you could consider a village, and planned to catalog as many types of animalia as possible in one week. We encountered birds, reptiles, and primitive hominoids. As our sniper was targeting one of these hominoids, we were trapped in a rudimentary net. We immediately used our plasma cutters to free ourselves, but then we lost consciousness.

The four of us woke to blinding light, and we were in slings, completely naked. Our arms and legs were bound tightly with leather straps and buckles.

Their leader walked in with a plastic mask that resembled a ghost, screaming. In his hand was a round wooden rod with a hemispherical rubber ending. He said something to us in their native tongue. We had no idea what it was without our translators, but it sounded menacing. He walked over to Harold15 and placed the rod at the edge of his anus and shoved it in. Harold15 screamed in pain and passed out.

Evan145 demanded we be let go, but the attacker and his buddies just laughed at him. They went over and tickled his armpits and feet and Evan145 peed on himself.

I tried to tell them we came in peace. But they either didn't understand my communication, or they had a total disregard for it. Since I had spoken next, they turned their attention toward me. The hominoid I believed to be the leader pulled the stick out of Harold15's anus and gave it to another being who brought it over to me and wiped it on me and laughed. Then he put it in my anus.

I have never felt such pain in my entire life. I saw only white as I screamed. Not only did he insert it, but he oscillated it, in and out, over and over, until I was crying and begging them to stop. After what seemed like minutes of torture, the leader told him to pull it out.

They got to work on Evan145 and saved Catherine23x for last.

I was particularly concerned about how they would treat our only female. I feared for her more than the others. But when it came time, she defiantly told them to go ahead, if that's how they "...got their rocks off."

They sodomized Catherine23x no more and no less than us. They never touched her genitalia, or any of ours for that matter, and I was relieved.

They allowed us to dress, escorted us to our ship, and provided us a handwritten note, with the faith that we'd be able to decipher it. It was clear they were asking us to leave and never come back.

We returned to our home base and reported our findings to the general counsel. During the journey, we decoded the message, which was short and to the point. "We, the citizens of Earth, have been victims of alien probing for thousands of years, and we are sick of it. Let this encounter be a lesson that this practice is unwelcome and forbidden. Do not return until your scientific data collection practices improve."

Richard was nothing if not a creature of habit. He enjoyed every minute of his mundane life and liked the prescribed monotony of getting up at 5:30 a.m., going to bed at 11 p.m., and in between, eating the same thing every day for breakfast, lunch, and dinner. He moved his family from Texas to Arizona solely to avoid Daylight Saving Time.

His job was to approve expense reports for a large firm, which, in forty years, had changed little except from moving from a physical inbox to a software system. The company forced him to change his password every six months, and he found this chore disconcerting.

When Richard passed away, peacefully in his bed between the hours of 11 and 5:30, he went straight to Heaven. At the Pearly Gates, St. Peter scanned his book and shook his head. "Mr. Richard Roth, of Tucson, Arizona, you have lived a scrupulous life. You are automatically admitted, but I tell you, you will have to change your ways, or you will find Heaven a bit overwhelming. Your soul is connected to all other souls, and your experiences are guided by the collective. Our residents are not restricted by their physical limitations and predispositions as in the Natural World. One day you may be a dog, chasing unlimited bones and cats, and the next, flying around like a bird, seeing the most beautiful aerial views of our amazing landscapes."

Richard was starting to sweat....

St. Peter leaned over and whispered, "Of course, there's always Hell. All you have to do is to request a transfer, and your days will be filled with monotony and unquenchable tedium." At this, he opened the gates and shouted, "Next!"

Richard floated through the clouds and felt a strange tugging at him from all directions, as if a thousand kind beings were beckoning him to come with them. He wasn't sure what to choose, so he just let his heart guide him. Soon, he was in a cool white room, with peaceful Siberian tigers, and attendants in tunics serving the most delicious plump grapes.

He lay down on an exceedingly comfortable sofa and watched the tigers yawn and the attendants scurry about. "I could get used to this," thought Richard, as he dozed off to sleep.

He awoke in the middle of a County Fair, his nose filled with the scent of Apple Pie and Cinnamon, and he saw the largest Ferris wheel he had ever seen. He had proposed to his wife Josie on a Ferris wheel, albeit a much smaller one, and he decided to get on this one.

There were enough seats for everyone and no waiting in line, and when he got on, he felt a strange sensation of nostalgia. But the attractive woman across from him was not Josie, although she was similar in manner and dress. He didn't feel sad that she wasn't his wife, but, instead, comfortable in this woman's presence. Potentially, they would have a future in this new world.

No sooner had he thought that than he was transported to a sporting event, where everyone around him was cheering. He was dressed in orange, clearly not for the blue team, but he did not know the sport, or anyone around him, even though they seemed to know him well. He tried to play along, but this constant change was starting to wear on him. There was no sense of time, or order, or familiarity.

He recalled St. Peter's advice and dismissed it again. *Why would I want to go to Hell? But then again, this place is* overwhelming, *as St. Peter had put it.*

Everyone was cheering and high fiving, but as he surveyed the crowd, he saw a lady in glasses staring down at her feet, not reveling with the others. She looked just how he felt, and he made his way over to talk to her.

Her name was Jane (her friends called her Plain Jane) and she was having a hard time adjusting to Heaven. She confided in Richard that St. Peter had offered the same advice to her as to him.

"What do you think he meant by that?" Richard asked.

"I think he meant that some people or their souls just aren't cut out for the hustle and bustle of this place. I've already been to six places, and I haven't even been here an hour!"

"But Hell is eternal damnation, and burning fire, and, I don't know, agony."

Jane asked, "What did you do for a living?"

"I was an accountant. I approved expense reports."

"I worked in a tollbooth. Some people here," she motioned to the merrymakers surrounding them, "would say that's agony. Maybe we're cut out for agony. Maybe we thrive on agony."

"But I always knew I was a good person. And good people go to Heaven. It's a reward."

"Does this feel like a reward?"

"No, but surely it gets better."

"I'm going to take my chances with Hell. If it doesn't work out, maybe I can come ba—" and she was gone.

She was replaced by a huge cheering guy wearing orange, and Richard went back to his seat. He tried to figure out the game, but ended up dwelling more on the fate of Plain Jane, and if she had really gone to Hell, or had just been whisked off to another collective fantasy, not one of her choosing.

Hours in Heaven turned into days – and even though he wasn't tired, he missed his 11 p.m. bedtime and his old existence, however dreary it could appear to an outside observer. Perhaps Jane was in a "better place," as ridiculous as that sounded.

It was then, as he was on a pristine, exotic beach, somewhere in Heaven, that he made his wish to be taken to Hell. And he was there.

It was hot, but not unbearably so (he was from Texas and Arizona) and on that lonesome highway, without an adulterer or murderer in sight, he came upon a solitary toll booth, with a familiar face inside. It was Plain Jane.

She recognized him immediately, and she was smiling. She said that there was a place in Hell for everyone, and that she had gotten her old job back. Murderers and other villains were in the worst kinds of prisons, but others, like her, held meaningful jobs and did them day in and day out.

Unlike St. Peter, she had no book to check to admit Richard: all were welcome in Hell. However, she did have his assignment. She pointed Richard toward a particularly hideous crag in the distance. "Enjoy your stay. Maybe this is where you were meant to be."

Richard met with a demon supervisor who asked him to manage the records of all the other workers in Hell. It was a tedious assignment, but one that Richard was good at. As the reports rolled in, Richard efficiently tabulated and summarized. He lost track of time, and days became weeks, and weeks became years. There were always new souls in Hell to monitor. Sometimes, he had to account for a soul's exodus to Heaven; however, never once did he desire to join them.

After hundreds of years, Richard's efficacy got the attention of some upper demons and he was asked to track not only the workers, but also the prisoners.

Richard never hired any employees, being willing and able to work constantly at his job. He never even missed his 11 p.m. bedtime or his three square meals; *these were unnecessary and a waste of time when there were so many things to do.*

Thousands of years passed by, and Richard was keeping up with more souls than ever. He was also providing additional useful information to his superiors about some of the criminals that deserved more punishment, stats about the most effective and ineffective punishments, and rehabilitation data. Some of the condemned were getting out of bondage and even filled leadership ranks. The change in climate got the attention of the Devil himself, who, one exceptionally warm day, appeared before Richard.

"I have been hearing great things about your efficiency and manner," said Satan.

Richard barely looked up into the Supreme ruler's eyes, there was so much work to do.

"What would you like as a reward?" Satan asked.

"I would just like to keep doing my job here, forever, *Your Highness*."

"Are you sure you wouldn't like to join the High Council? Your ideas and methods are quite extraordinary." The Devil beamed with a diabolical smile.

"I would like more work, Your Highness. I would like to continue to track souls in Hell for all eternity."

"Done. And you can tell your friends, despite my tarnished reputation, I always keep my promises. Ah, but you haven't got any friends here, have you? Except maybe... Plain Jane?"

Richard stopped working. He hadn't thought about her in years.... "Is she still greeting the souls at the entrance to Hell?"

"Yes, and like you she wants nothing more. I would say that the two of you are the Best in Hell at what you do."

And Richard beamed with pride, for just a second, then resumed his work, as the Devil slipped away.

IQuit

March 5

I am starting to notice a decline in my cognitive abilities. I'm not sure if there will be a floor, or if I will just keep declining until I am in a vegetative state. So, I am going to keep a journal to document this. It might help others who are dealing with this condition as a patient or a supporter.

Some background: I could read at age two. I learned French at age four. My parents had me take an IQ test when I was seven. It was easy. Said my IQ was 170. But I'm not sure test makers know how to make tests for IQ's above 150 for seven-year-olds.

On subsequent tests I knew what they were going to ask before they asked it, and I often found flaws in the questioning.

No matter. I went to college at thirteen, could have gone at ten, easy. Majored in Electrical Engineering and then decided to go to Med School: a regular Doogie Howser. I worked as a doctor from my twenties to my mid-forties, and I enjoyed a great career, got married, had two beautiful and successful children, and that's when things started going bad.

A lot of my success has been due to my ability to find new and unique ways to treat patients. I don't believe in a "one size fits all" mentality. Environment, financial situations, health habits, are all data points that medical professionals should consider. And I was consciously and unconsciously evaluating all these factors in determining treatment plans.

I was aware of my dysfunction after a specific incident. A woman, sixty-five years old, was exhibiting shortness of breath and frequent blackouts. I was able to narrow the symptoms down to a few possible causes, but when I added in her social situation I was confounded. Not only did her situation not help analyze her problem, but I was also not sure why I was taking into account her social situation at all. It was like someone else told me to do it, but I wasn't sure how to follow the instructions.

It wasn't just that. I was walking down the street and spotted a quarter on the sidewalk. The old me would have questioned why it was there and not already picked up, but I reached for it anyway, and it was glued to the ground. A kid with a phone was recording it and laughing. I laughed too, but secretly I was disappointed that I didn't see an obvious gag that was laid out in front of me in plain sight.

Thinking something was off with my brain, I decided to get tested. My IQ came back fifteen points lower than the worst score I had ever received. I expected that different tests might be skewed, but also undoubtedly something was wrong with me, so I re-tested: to the exact same score.

There was one question in particular that I could not figure out. It looked familiar to me, but I could not reason the answer. What was more frustrating than not knowing the answer was knowing that I previously could have worked the problem. I knew my abstract reasoning was failing, and with it my career.

I was confused as to how this could happen, and I spent an inordinate amount of time looking into my past dietary habits, social habits, etc. I treated myself as a patient, but I was unable to determine a root cause for this slip in my acuity. I spent hundreds of hours poring through scientific evaluations on loss of reasoning and as I was doing this I began to understand less and less of what I was reading. Like things that were never too technical to understand were now arduous. I tried a variety of supplements and drugs to try to compensate for my mental deficiency, but I could tell I was still getting "dumber." I sought out a colleague of mine in Manchester, England who was researching the relationship between age and IQ and he agreed that I exhibited an extraordinary decline in my mental faculties with no clear medical explanation. Over twelve weeks he tested me and collected empirical data to substantiate the decline.

As partners now, he did not hold back in presenting these findings to me, though toward the end of our tenure, it was harder and harder for me to understand the intricacies and nuances of his data. He was a kind soul, though, and explained the information in intermediate terms until I was able to internalize it.

We concluded that, for whatever reason, I am rapidly losing the ability to make cognitive connections.

At this point, here is what I fear: I will most certainly not be able to practice medicine much longer. I have already lost my unique ability to diagnose complex predicaments, and I think I will soon be unable to diagnose even the most obvious remedies. I am becoming ordinary, and the trajectory is to something lesser.

I will not be able to provide for my family, but I will string along my talents as far as they will get me even if I must take a demotion. I believe I can manage for some time, although the future is quite unknown. Perhaps my cells are exponentially declining, in which case I may be out of a job in three to six months.

June 16

I am working as a brick layer. I like being outdoors. I am able to match the pattern, but I often need help with the corners. Judy says I'm not stressed like I used to be.

I'm glad I have Judy, and the kids are all supportive of me. It seems now like my whole other life was temporary, and this is my life now. Imagine that I was a doctor!

I don't like taking the tests anymore. But I do. Doctor Frederick says I'm doing fine, but I don't ask what the scores are. I know I'm still getting dumber. Today I put the milk in the bowl and then the cereal. *Who does that?*

September 10

Today is September tenth. This is Judy Hamilton, and I am writing in Craig's diary. He wanted to have this diary for the kids so they could understand how he was feeling as his memory failed him. He doesn't have Alzheimer's, but I think what he has is worse. He lost his job as a bricklayer about two months ago, and I told him just to come home and be with us. He watches some TV and likes to play the puzzle where you put shapes in the holes of a box. He has trouble distinguishing the two triangles, but I think he is the happiest he's ever been. He loves it when the kids wrestle with him and when the old Looney Toons cartoons come on, especially The Roadrunner. He says "Meep Meep" a lot. I will love him as long as he's here on earth with us.

October 25

This week, we had to move Craig to a hospital specializing in care for the "profoundly handicapped." He cannot feed, bathe, or go potty by himself. The hospital is an hour and a half away, but I visit every day, and the kids go to see him at least three times a week. They know he didn't choose to be this way. We are going to give him as much love as we can, now and forever.

November 2

Craig passed away in his sleep. We are not sure what the cause was, but maybe his brain just quit.

I like that explanation. It makes sense to me and the kids. A year ago, Craig would have never accepted an explanation like that. But I think now he'd also be good with it. Craig will forever be missed.

Love,

Judy, Kenny, George, Marta, and Elizabeth

THE SONG AT THE END

We were in the last stages of the war. The Legunos, having already overrun the larger cities, were invading outlying rural communities like ours. I could have tried to flee on horseback, but my whole stable lay slain in the corral with buzzards picking at their hides.

The insurgents took a few prisoners to their makeshift camp at the elementary school, bordering the far side of my property. The only reason for them to take hostages was to trade for something, so I rationalized my only hope of survival was to become a hostage myself.

I vaulted the three-foot high fence that separated my pasture from the school campus, and scurried across the playground to the closest building. Carefully peering in the window, I could see a group of my neighbors in a classroom, about half with black bags over their heads.

An armed guard came around the corner and spotted me. Instead of running, I acted as if I was a hostage that had managed to escape. He ziptied me and led me in the back door where I joined the others.

A lieutenant arrived with more black bags and started bagging the rest of us. I suspect there was only enough for the number of people originally captured when a lady cried out, "He just got here! Take him!" which was either not understood or unheeded. She was dragged, kicking and screaming, out to the playground where she was executed.

I stayed silent, wondering how long we would be kept or what the execution schedule might be. Perhaps we were not hostages, but so far my plan was working – I was still one of the few alive.

Over the next few hours, the guards took us in groups of five to use the restroom and to eat some dried snacks which looked like army rations or space food.

One lady in my group accused me of getting her friend Carol killed. She said it should have been me, which was totally true. I told her if it made her feel any better, I would be the next volunteer. At that time, I wasn't sure if I was telling the truth, but it felt like the right thing to say.

Toward the end of the day, they removed the bags over our heads for good. I didn't understand the point of having them in the first place, but maybe it was just to control the headcount. Wendy, Carol's friend, took the opportunity to tell the rest of the hostages that I had agreed to be the next victim.

I corrected her, saying I would be the first volunteer, if we needed to produce one. The rest seemed OK with that distinction. My new strategy was to be the first hostage released for the most important Leguno captive.

Our captors treated us well, but Wendy was getting on my nerves. I was daydreaming that they'd shoot her next, when the lieutenant came back, and in broken English, said, "I need bollunteer." I raised my hand and the others either nodded their approval or looked away.

As we left the room, Wendy told me to "Rot in Hell."

I wasn't sure if my plan was working, but instead of being taken to the playground like Carol, I was taken to the music room which had been turned into a command post.

This was where I met the leader – a short Leguno woman with a mild disposition. She spoke clear English and was calmly dictating terms for the exchange of hostages. I was made to kneel on the ground at gunpoint while she finished her conversations.

"Mr. Bloncki, I am told you volunteered for this – very admirable. But it looks like we have had an unforeseen setback and one of our agents has died at the hands of your government. For this reason, we are going to execute you. I am sorry."

Off to the side, I see the shadow of a pistol pointed at the shadow of my head and know my time is up.

I feel the bullet go in, and as I am falling in slow motion, I feebly attempt to wave goodbye with a limp right arm.

As I fall onto my face, a song I've never heard before is playing inside my obliterated brain – a pre-recorded, over-simplified, unfitting end to a long, complex, beautiful life that will never happen again.

"It's the end of the road

...another life is over."

Dear Reader,

Thank you so much for reading Back End of the Bell Curve. Did you enjoy it? Please let me know by leaving a review.

Ending too sad? Start over with Henry the Horse, check out the cover art on the last page, or visit www.phillbradley.com for additional stories.

Best regards,

Phill

INSIDERS

Would you like the chance to read stories from the next collection early?

Find out when the next collection is out?

Use the QR code below to be an insider and **get one bonus story for joining***

* Totally free - just need a name and valid email address

BETA READERS

When joining the Insiders mailing list, you can indicate if you are interested in joining the Beta Reader Program. Spots are limited, but I will let you know if you are accepted. Beta Readers have access to most new works before they are published.

More on the Beta Reader program can be found at www.phillbradley.com.

Back End of the Bell Curve Short Story Cover Art

Short story cover art by Phill Bradley and Meagan Smith.

AI used to generate portions of some cover images, but not Henry.